The Missing Newspaper Caper

Hilda Stahl

ACCENT BOOKS
Denver, Colorado

ACCENT BOOKS

A division of Accent Publications, Inc.
12100 West Sixth Avenue
P.O. Box 15337
Denver, Colorado 80215

Library of Congress Catalog Card Number 86-71178

ISBN 0-89636-221-3

Dedicated with love to
Mike, Kathie & Molly Deasy

Meet Wren, Bess, Tim, Paula—and their families—as they unravel mysteries and find that serving Christ means putting love into action.

Wren House - Her father's a detective, her mother a lawyer. She wants to be just like her dad, and finds mystery—and trouble—everywhere.

Bess Talbot - Wren's best friend and almost next door neighbor. The cautious one, Bess nevertheless finds herself drawn into Wren's mysteries.

Tim Avery - At first a thorn in Wren's side, Tim soon shows his ability as a detective. Through him Wren and Bess learn some valuable lessons about Christianity.

Paula Gantz - The neighborhood troublemaker, she delights in getting Wren into trouble. But she, too, plays an important part in the mystery.

All four are in fifth grade at Jordan Christian Academy. Join their eager, enthusiastic enjoyment of life, each other, and the adventure of growing up in Christ.

Contents

1.
A New Project

Wren House lifted her jacket collar up to keep out the chilly October wind. Her blue skirt pressed against her cold legs as she walked down the sidewalk. "Can't you walk faster, Bess? We don't want to be late for school."

Bess Talbot lifted her chin. The tip of her nose was as red as her cheeks. "I can't run and talk at the same time, you know."

"I didn't say run. I said walk fast."

Bess shrugged and walked a little faster. "What's wrong with you today, Wren? You're not being very nice to me."

Wren sighed heavily. "Mom told me this morning that I have to start taking piano lessons."

Bess stopped short. Her blue eyes sparkled. "That's wonderful!"

Wren shook her head. "It is not."

"But you love music."

"I know, but I don't want to use my time for piano

7

lessons and practice." Wren strode forward and Bess was forced to run to keep up with her. "Mom wants to make sure I don't have time for detective work."

"Oh, Wren."

"She doesn't want me to solve mysteries. She thinks I spend too much time poking my nose into other people's business."

"She's right, you know."

Wren stopped short and frowned. "I do not!"

"Well, don't fight with me! I'm not making you take piano lessons."

"Sorry." Wren walked along in silence, her head full of all the arguments she'd given Mom for not taking piano lessons. She knew none of them would work. As a lawyer Mom knew all about arguing a case without giving in. Once Mom made up her mind about something, she stuck with it.

Bess took a deep breath and changed the subject. She didn't like to see Wren unhappy. "I wonder what the great surprise is that Miss Brewster will tell us about today?"

"What surprise?" said Paula Gantz from behind them.

Wren whipped around and frowned. Had Paula heard what she'd said about piano lessons? If Paula knew, soon the entire school would know, maybe the entire town. "Don't sneak up on us, Paula!"

Paula pushed between the two girls. "Who says I was sneaking?"

8

Wren shrugged, and her shoulders sagged. She didn't want to fight, not even with Paula.

Bess slowed her pace. "Paula, *you* should know the secret project all the teachers at Jordan Christian Academy are going to tell us about today."

"Well, I don't know." Paula tossed her head, then peered closely at Wren. "But what about you, Wren? You're supposed to be the great detective. You're supposed to find out everything about everything. Didn't you learn the secret?"

Wren stiffened. Her brown eyes snapped. "I don't spy on teachers, Paula Gantz!"

"Did I say spy?" Paula looked very innocent.

"Do you know the secret, Wren?" asked Bess. "As your very best friend I think I have a right to know what you found out."

"I already told you that I don't know. And I don't spy on people. Not unless I'm on a case."

Paula laughed and Wren's face turned red.

"Let's go before we're late." Wren dashed down the sidewalk toward the brick building that was Jordan Christian Academy during the week and their church on Sundays. She didn't want Paula or Bess to remind her of the times she'd thought she'd found a mystery to solve only to learn differently.

"Wait for me!" Bess held her carefully brushed blond hair to keep the wind from blowing it out of place as she ran with Wren. She wanted to look nice in case Wren's brother, Neil, said hello to her.

"I hope you're both late!" shouted Paula as she lagged behind.

When she reached the school Wren watched for Brian Davies, but he wasn't standing with the group of eighth grade boys near the door. Her heart sank, then lifted with excitement as she caught sight of him just outside the eighth grade room. Just seeing him was enough, but speaking to him would make her day special. Before she reached him, he stepped into the room.

"Too bad," whispered Bess.

Wren nodded. Bess knew her secret admiration for Brian just as she knew Bess's secret about Neil.

Several minutes later Wren sat at her desk, her hands locked together, and forced her mind off piano lessons and even off Brian Davies. She leaned forward to catch every word that Miss Brewster was saying.

"This will be an all school paper." Miss Brewster said as she flipped back her long brown curls with the back of her slender hand, then walked across the front of the room. Her black skirt touched the top of her high black boots. Her black jacket swung open to show flashes of her silky red blouse. "We want our fifth grade to have outstanding articles. We want people to want to buy our paper and after they buy it, we want them to enjoy it."

Paula Gantz shot her arm high into the air and waved it wildly.

Miss Brewster frowned slightly. "Yes, Paula."

"I'll make a good reporter, Miss Brewster. I know how to get a lot of news for us to print."

Wren groaned deep inside herself. Paula always knew everything about everybody, even the things nobody wanted known.

Miss Brewster nodded. "Thank you, Paula."

Wren shot a look at Bess and Bess bobbed her eyebrows. Bess knew all about Paula's nosiness. Everyone in all of Jordan Christian Academy knew, even Miss Brewster. Probably everyone in the entire state of Michigan knew.

"The paper will come out once a week," continued Miss Brewster as she sank back against her desk with her hands pressed on either side of her. "We'll have school news, national news, and city news as well as heartwarming articles about people helping people." Miss Brewster pushed away from the desk and stood with her hands in her pockets and a broad smile on her pretty face. The aroma of her perfume blended together with the smell of chalk dust and coffee from the teacher's lounge down the hall.

"You'll all sell subscriptions to the paper. With the money we'll buy a new copy machine for JCA." She beamed a smile around the room. "The class that sells the most subscriptions will put on a program for the rest of the school as well as parents and friends."

Wren's heart leaped. She loved singing for everyone.

"We have twenty students and four divisions to cover, so that means we'll have groups of five to work together on each project."

Tim Avery caught Wren's eye and she nodded. She knew he wanted to work with her. They worked well together since they both loved solving mysteries.

Tim raised his hand. His freckles stood out boldly on his face. His red hair was combed neatly.

"Yes, Tim."

"I want to be in Wren's group."

"So do I," said Bess quickly.

"That's three of you," said Miss Brewster, writing the names on a paper on her desk. "You need two more. How about you, Sean?"

Sean flushed to the roots of his blond hair. "I guess so."

Paula's hand shot up. "Me, too, Miss Brewster."

Wren groaned. She knew Paula wanted in their group only because of Sean Riley. Working with Paula would be terrible—worse than terrible.

Miss Brewster answered the others who waved their arms for attention, wrote down the groups, then said, "I'll assign each group a topic. Wren, your group will do articles on people helping people since you did such a wonderful job on the movie that we did a few weeks ago."

Wren smiled. She liked that topic the best, but it would've been interesting to do city news also.

Miss Brewster assigned the other topics with a flourish. "Each group meet together in different parts of the room and discuss your first assignment. Today is Wednesday. The story must be on my desk by Tuesday of next week to give the high school students time to have them ready to sell by Friday."

"We'll be ready," said Paula.

Miss Brewster nodded. "Also, I want you to be thinking of a name for the paper. We want it to be outstanding and eye-catching."

"How about the *JCA News*," said Bess, and everyone groaned. She looked around with a hurt expression on her face. "Well?"

"It's certainly specific," said Miss Brewster kindly. "And everyone will have an opportunity to enter a name. But you're excused into your groups now."

The noise of moving desks and shuffling feet filled the room as Wren led the way to the corner of the room near the aquarium. She sat at the table with Bess on one side of her and Tim the other. Paula made sure she sat beside Sean. He moved away from her a little and she scowled at him.

Wren cleared her throat. "Why don't we each find a story and then write it out. After that we can get together and put the best parts of each person's story together to make the finished story that we hand in."

"We could talk to Amos Pike and see if he has an idea for a story," said Tim.

"I remember him," said Sean. "He was in the movie you did."

Tim nodded. "He was, and he loves to help."

"I think we should ask my dad," said Paula. She looked right at Sean. "He's a doctor, you know. He helps people all the time."

"I know," said Sean, moving restlessly.

Wren looked up at the ceiling. Paula never let anyone forget that her dad was a doctor.

"I think we should interview several people, and then vote on the story we want to write," said Tim.

"Good idea, Tim." Wren looked around the table. "Do you all agree?"

Bess nodded. Paula waited until Sean did, then she did too.

Bess pulled out a pencil and paper. "I write the neatest, so I'll make the list." She tapped the tip of the pencil on her paper. "Now, tell me who we should ask about a story."

Wren wrinkled her brow and thought while the others named off people. Several names went through her mind, but she didn't say anything.

"Wren?" asked Bess.

"I want to think about it. I don't know who to say."

"I bet you'll say your dad," said Paula. "You

think he's so great because he's a detective." She made detective sound like a bad word.

Wren doubled her fists in her lap and tightened her jaw. "I just might."

Paula leaned forward with a wicked chuckle. "Or you could interview yourself, Bird House." Paula lifted her hands, palms out and fingers spread. "Fifth Grade Detective Does Good Work While Taking Dreaded Piano Lessons."

Paula had heard! Wren pressed her lips tightly together as she forced back her anger.

"I don't think you should tease Wren," said Sean. "You're mean, Paula."

Paula's eyes widened as she stared at Sean.

"I think you should apologize," continued Sean.

"I think you're ugly and mean, Sean Riley!" Paula twisted in her seat and waved her arm high. "Miss Brewster, Miss Brewster."

"Yes, Paula."

"They're being mean to me."

"What?" they all said together.

"Now, Paula," said Miss Brewster. She walked to the table and looked down at them. "You must learn to work together peacefully."

Paula lifted her rounded chin. "Wren's mad because her mom's making her take piano lessons; Tim's mad because his mom is still in some hospital to stop drinking, and Bess and Sean hate me!"

15

"Don't say another word about my mom!" cried Tim.

"You should've stayed in public school, Paula!" snapped Wren.

Paula glared at Wren, then looked up at Miss Brewster with a pleading look on her face. "I don't want to be in this group. Let me be in a different one."

Four heads nodded in agreement. "Put her in a different group," Sean said.

Miss Brewster rested her hands on her slender waist. "It's too late to change groups. You know it's just as important to learn to get along as it is to help others."

Wren's heart sank, but she knew Miss Brewster was right.

Bess and Wren exchanged long looks before Bess said slowly, "Okay. We'll try."

Tim and Sean nodded, but didn't say anything.

Paula's face turned brick red. "I don't want to work with this group. I won't work with them!"

Miss Brewster's lips thinned. "Paula, I'm sorry if you're unhappy, but you asked to be in this group, and you must stay in it. I'm sure if you try, you'll be able to get along with your classmates. And Wren, Bess, Tim, Sean, I want you to be kind to Paula." Miss Brewster looked sternly at them and walked to a group at the other end of the room.

Paula glared at the others and crossed her arms. "Well, I just won't do any of the work. So there!"

"And we won't put your name on the story with ours," said Tim.

Paula poked out her bottom lip in a pout.

"Stop being a baby, Paula," said Bess.

"I don't think I want to do this," said Sean.

Wren sank lower in her chair. She didn't feel much like writing a great story for the paper either. She didn't like it when they all fussed with each other. Besides, she'd much rather go home and watch her dad be a detective.

2.
A Search for News

On the way home from school the next day, Wren, Bess, Sean, and Tim stopped their bikes outside the public library. "I think we should talk to Mrs. Elwood," Wren said. "We couldn't find anything yesterday and she sometimes tells interesting stories that really happened."

"I should've brought my book back," said Bess, looking worried. "It's due tomorrow."

"You can bring it back tomorrow then," said Wren. "It's only three blocks from your house."

"I know. I just don't want Mrs. Elwood to think that I forgot my book."

"She's not going to notice." Wren pushed her hands into her jacket pockets.

"I still think I'd rather wait out here," said Bess.

"She won't notice!" cried Wren impatiently.

Sean raced Tim up the wide, stone steps to the front door. Wren followed and finally Bess dashed after them. She caught the heavy wooden door just before it swung shut. Light shone through the high narrow windows. Smells of paper and dust hung in the air.

Mrs. Elwood stood behind the front desk and peered through her glasses at them. She wore a brown suit with a white blouse. Her white hair curled around her narrow face. "Hello. I didn't expect you children today. Saturdays are your usual days."

Wren stepped forward, hooking her dark hair behind her ears. "We came for a story."

"A story?"

Tim quickly told Mrs. Elwood about the school project. "Do you know of a good story about people helping people?"

Mrs. Elwood tapped the eraser of her pencil on the desk near the checkout cards. "I did hear that Steve Bushnell loaned his car to the Garnets until they could get theirs repaired."

"What's so big about that?" asked Bess.

"Bob Garnet couldn't get to work to earn a living if he didn't have a car," said Mrs. Elwood. "And if he couldn't earn a living then his family would go without food and a home."

Wren jotted down the names. "We'll check into it. Thanks, Mrs. Elwood."

"That's quite all right." Mrs. Elwood turned to Bess and peered down at her. "Don't you have a book due?"

Bess shot a knowing look at Wren before she managed a smile for Mrs. Elwood. "It's due tomorrow." Her voice cracked slightly and her face turned a brighter red than Tim's hair as she walked toward the door.

Outdoors Tim said, "I don't think we're going to find a great story very easily."

"I told you I shouldn't have gone in," said Bess.

"Forget it," said Wren, frowning.

"I thought it would be simple," said Sean. "I always hear good stories."

"I think we should forget the one Mrs. Elwood told us," said Tim. "It's not spectacular enough."

"Let's get the *Jordan News* and see if there's something in it," said Bess.

"But that's reported news," Sean objected as he picked up his bike. "We have to find something that isn't already reported."

"We won't give up. We still have to see Amos Pike," said Tim.

"Let's go visit him now." Wren led the way and they rode fast to Amos's little house.

Buster barked just inside the door and wriggled happily as the four children walked up the porch steps. Amos opened the door wide and beamed with pleasure.

"Come in. I baked cookies today just in case you youngsters came over." Amos hiked up his pants and pulled his sweater down in place. "Chocolate drop cookies." He stopped suddenly and peered at Sean. "Have I met you?"

Sean nodded. "At school. When you came to see the movies. I'm Sean Riley."

"Glad to see you again, Sean. Anything special bring you all here?"

Wren kept her hand on Buster's small head. "We're starting a newspaper at school. And our assignment is to write a story about people helping people."

"Sounds great to me." Amos set out the cookies and filled glasses with water. "It'd be good to read a paper like that instead of one filled with bad news."

"Can you help us?" asked Tim.

Amos rubbed his wrinkled cheek. "I might be able to. Let me think."

"We want something really great," said Bess. She peered in the mirror near the kitchen door and smoothed her hair into place. "Something out of the ordinary."

Amos narrowed his eyes thoughtfully. "I heard about a guy that bought a week's worth of groceries for a family down the block."

"That's nice," said Tim.

"But we want something more," said Bess.

Wren ate a cookie and drank her water as she listened to Amos talk. He usually did most of the talking when they visited him. Dad had said that Amos was lonely and that's why he talked so much while they were there. Wren didn't mind at all.

Later they said goodbye and rode down the street to talk with Gloria Meecker, a woman that Bess had suggested. She wasn't home.

"Let's try the next name on our list," said Sean. He pulled the list away from Bess. "Jake Cradox."

But Jake couldn't help them at all. As they rode away from his house Bess sighed heavily. "This is getting boring."

"I thought it would be easy," said Sean.

"We can't give up yet," said Tim.

In the park Wren tied her jacket sleeves around her waist and let the breeze blow against her hot body. She wiped perspiration off her upper lip and forehead as she turned to the others. "We don't have anything yet. Any suggestions?"

Sean laid his bike beside Wren's and shook his head. "I have to go home soon even if we don't find anything interesting."

Wren knew he lived only two blocks from her and that he was expected at home to help with his little brothers. Her face lit up. "Let's go talk to your mother, Sean. She's always helping people. And you always help her."

"That's boring," said Bess.

Wren frowned at Bess and Bess looked hurt.

"I think it's a good idea," said Tim. Talking to Amos Pike hadn't helped and Tim was ready to try anything. "What is your mom doing today?"

Sean rubbed a suntanned hand over his blond

hair and looked embarrassed. "I don't know what she's doing. Last night she typed business letters for Dad."

Bess turned away. "Boring, boring."

Wren jabbed Bess in the back, but kept her eyes on Sean. "We can ask her and then we'll know if it'll make a good article."

"Let's go!" Tim picked up the ten-speed that Adam Landon had bought him last year.

Wren bent down to pick up her bike just in time to see a movement in the bushes nearby. She bit her lower lip and narrowed her dark eyes.

"What's wrong?" asked Bess.

"I saw something in the bushes," Wren whispered.

Bess studied the bushes for several seconds. "I don't see anything. Let's go. You are not going to start doing detective work while we're trying to get a story."

Wren crept toward the bushes, then leaped around them. "I thought so! Paula, are you spying on us?"

Paula slowly stood, her face red. She lifted her chin defiantly. "I changed my mind and I'm going to get the story with you. So there!" She stared from one to the other as if to dare them to send her away. No one did.

"We're going to Sean's house," said Tim.

"I heard," said Paula.

"So, you *were* spying!" cried Bess.

"I was not!"

"Then what were you doing?" asked Wren.

Paula rubbed her hands down her jeans and moved restlessly. She licked her lips. "So what if I was spying? I only wanted to find out what was happening. I do belong to this group, you know."

"You said you wouldn't work with us," said Sean.

Paula looked down at the ground, then lifted her head to look right at Sean. "I changed my mind. Women can do that, you know."

Tim groaned and Wren walked away.

Later at Sean's house Wren drank a tall glass of water. The ice cubes clinked against the sides of the glass. Sean's five-year-old brothers chattered nonstop at her feet. They were the first triplets she'd ever seen and they looked almost alike with blond hair and eyes like Sean's.

"Did you ask your mother where she was going?" Tim stepped back from one of the little boys who wanted to touch him with a hand smeared with peanut butter.

Sean nodded. "She's going to the park to be alone for awhile."

"So much for a story," said Bess.

Paula bent down to one of the boys. "What's your name?"

"Ronnie." His R sounded like a W. "That's Bobby and that's Jimmy."

"My dad delivered you," Paula said, puffing her

chest out importantly. "Did you know that? He's a doctor. You're the first and only triplets he's ever delivered."

Ronnie fell on his brothers and wrestled over the kitchen floor.

"How long do you have to watch the boys?" asked Tim.

Sean shrugged. "Not too long. Maybe an hour."

Tim rolled his eyes. "I could never take care of them that long. I think we should write a story about you helping your mom by taking care of your brothers."

"Boring," whispered Bess with a quick look to see if Wren had heard.

"I always wanted brothers," said Paula in a strange voice. "But there's just me."

Wren bit her tongue to keep from saying that one Paula Gantz was more than enough. "We can write the story down, but we'll keep trying to find another one."

"We need something exciting." Bess walked away from the sink toward the table, stopped, and flung out her arms. "Doesn't anyone know someone that saved a lot of people from burning up in a fire?"

"No," said Wren.

"How about someone who fed a starving country?"

"Give up, Bess," said Tim.

"I was only trying to help." Bess walked to the door. "I'm going home. Are you coming, Wren?"

Wren nodded. "I guess so. See you all tomorrow."

"I'm going too," said Paula. She grabbed her jacket and ran out after Wren and Bess.

"This is harder than I thought," said Bess. "I can't believe we don't know anyone that's done something great."

Wren climbed on her bike and pedaled away. Right now she felt like giving up. "But I won't," she declared softly. Mom and Dad had told her often that once she'd started a job or a project that she had to finish it. They said it helped build character. She sighed heavily and muttered, "I should have a very strong character by now." She wrinkled her nose and pedaled harder.

3.
Frantic Phone Call

Wren stood outside her back door with Bess. Paula had gone home, and Wren suddenly felt very tired and bored. "Are you coming in?"

Bess nodded. "I can't stay long, but I want to see Neil. Is he home?"

Wren shrugged. Sometimes she got tired of Bess and her feelings for Neil.

Bess patted her hair and tugged her jacket down. "Do I look all right?"

"You look fine."

Wren walked through the back porch to the kitchen. The faint sound of music drifted from Dad's office. His office at home had an outside entrance as well as a connecting door inside the house. When the inner door was closed Wren knew he had a client and that she couldn't disturb him. A hint of frying bacon hung in the air. Wren draped her jacket over a kitchen chair. "I'd like to have a school newspaper but I wonder if we'll ever find a

27

story to write."

"I don't know." Bess glanced around for any sign of Neil. "We didn't find anything today either."

"We could pray that we find something soon." Wren and Bess often prayed together for answers to problems. Wren had learned long ago that God answered prayer.

"I'll pray." Bess stood near the sink with Wren beside her.

"Heavenly Father, thank you for caring about every part of our lives. Help us to find a story that's not boring. And help us to write it well. Thank you. In Jesus' name, Amen."

"Amen," said Wren with a smile. "I think when we try tomorrow we'll find a story."

Bess nodded. "A really great story!"

"Right."

"I'll ask Mom. She meets a lot of people while she's selling houses." Bess touched a glass on the counter beside the sink. Neil might have had a drink of water from that very glass. "Mom said that she just sold a house to Simon Cole. He's new around here. They lived in Lansing, I think, and have two boys. Jason, the eight-year-old, has really big problems, and Mr. Cole wanted to move to the country to see if it would help him."

Wren lifted her head in sudden interest. "What problems?"

"It's not a mystery, Wren."

"How do you know?"

"I just know."

Wren sighed. "I wish something really exciting would happen."

Bess looked around for Neil. "So do I."

"I feel like doing detective work right now."

"Don't let your mother hear you say that."

Wren touched the back of a kitchen chair and looked at the plants hanging around the window over the sink. "If I could find a mystery that needed to be solved, I'd drop everything and solve it."

Bess locked her hands behind her. "Where *is* Neil?"

"I would pit my brilliant mind against the unsolvable problem and I'd win!"

Bess peeked out the door and down the hallway that led to the bedrooms. "Maybe he's working on his computer."

Wren sank to a chair and rested her elbows on the table with her chin in her hands. "I'd crack the case within hours after I started working on it."

Bess turned with a frown. "What are you talking about, Wren House?"

Wren jumped up. "About living! I can't survive without a mystery to solve!"

"Oh, Wren!"

The phone rang and Wren dashed across the room. She lifted the receiver with a breathless hello.

"Wren?"

"Yes?"

"This is Mina Thomkins. Amos said I should call you."

Wren frowned. Why would Amos say that? She had just seen Amos about an hour ago.

"I need you, Wren." The little old lady sounded frantic. "I'm at the end of my rope. Could you come see me right away? Amos said you could help me."

Had her grandson neglected the lawn again? Maybe she was lonely and just wanted to talk. But why did she sound so upset? "Help with what?"

"A mystery."

Wren's heart leaped and her dark eyes lit up. Had she heard right? Was she dreaming? She gripped the receiver tighter. "A mystery?"

"Oh, no," said Bess with a groan.

Wren ignored her. "What kind of mystery?"

"Come right over and I'll tell you."

"I'll be there in five minutes." Wren slammed down the receiver and spun around to Bess. "I have a case to solve! My first case that someone asked me to solve!"

"Don't forget what your mom said."

"About what?"

"Being a detective. You know she doesn't want you to get involved in mysteries."

"She likes me to help others. And Mina Thomkins needs my help." Wren tipped back her head and shouted at the top of her lungs, "Yahoo!"

Bess flushed and backed away. Sometimes Wren

acted really strange.

Neil ran into the kitchen. "What's going on with you, Wren?"

Bess stepped away from Wren so Neil wouldn't think she had shouted also. "Hi, Neil."

"Hi." Neil glanced at Bess, then faced Wren. "Why'd you yell?"

Wren gripped Neil's arm and pumped it up and down. "I have a mystery to solve, Neil. A real one. For Mina Thomkins, that woman who lives on Maple Street that I told you about."

Neil unhooked Wren's fingers. "I happen to like that arm."

"A real mystery, Neil!"

"She's excited," said Bess.

Wren twirled around. "My first real case!"

Neil walked to the door, then looked back. "Don't forget to get home in time to help with dinner. It is your turn, you know."

Wren shook her head and groaned. How could she waste time helping with dinner? "Will you take my turn, Neil?"

"No way!"

"Please?" Wren clasped her hands together near her chin and widened her brown eyes.

"I already took so many of your turns that if you tried to catch up you'd be doing the work every day for two months."

"Just this once, Neil?"

"You always say that."

31

"Please?"

Neil pushed his sleeves up and stood with his hands on his hips. "No."

Wren stepped closer and looked as pathetic as she could. "This really is the last time I'll ask."

"Oh, sure."

Wren put on her most pleading look. "I mean it this time."

"I don't think you should ask him," said Bess.

"Thanks, Bess," said Neil with a smile.

Bess sagged weakly against the table and couldn't say another word. Neil had said thanks to her! He had smiled at her!

Wren tossed her head. "Oh, all right! I'll be back in time to help with dinner." Wren ran to the door. "Coming, Bess?"

Bess hesitated. She wanted to look at Neil just a little longer, but he walked out of the room so she ran after Wren.

Wren pedaled as fast as she could all the way to Maple Street, her heart leaping. She wanted to stop everyone on the street and tell them that she had her very first case.

At Mrs. Thomkins's house Wren hit the sidewalk on the run, leaving Bess far behind. She reached out to ring the doorbell and the door burst open.

"Wren! You came!" Mrs. Thomkins grabbed Wren's arm and tugged her inside.

4.
The Case

"What's the mystery, Mrs. Thomkins?" Wren tried to make her voice sound very professional, but excitement crept in anyway. Her cheeks were flushed and her eyes glowed.

"Let's sit down first, dear." Mrs. Thomkins looked ready to collapse. She was short and slight and her white face was lined with wrinkles. But her gray blouse and dark blue slacks were crisp and neat. She sank down on a kitchen chair and wrapped her hands around the cup of coffee that apparently she'd been drinking before Wren came.

Wren draped her jacket over a chair and sank to the edge of it. She smelled the coffee and Mrs. Thomkins's cologne. Before Mrs. Thomkins could speak, the back doorbell rang.

"Now, who could that be?"

Wren leaped up with a giggle. "I forgot about Bess. She came with me. My friend, Bess Talbot.

You met her before. I'll let her in."

"Thank you, Wren. I really am too exhausted to get up again."

Wren ran to the door and opened it for Bess.

Bess stepped inside with a pained expression on her face. "Wren, you didn't wait for me."

"I'm sorry."

"Come in, Bess," said Mrs. Thomkins from where she sat at the table. "I was just getting ready to tell Wren about the terrible mystery."

A shiver of delight ran down Wren's spine. "A terrible mystery?"

"I don't know why I came," said Bess with a long sigh.

"I'm sure you'll want to help your friend." Mrs. Thomkins patted Bess's arm as she sat at the table.

"I guess so," said Bess.

Wren perched on the edge of her chair. "Now, tell us about the mystery." Her eyes sparkled and the words sounded like drops of pure gold to her.

Mrs. Thomkins pushed a wrinkled hand to her throat. "It really is quite mysterious."

Wren trembled.

"Maybe I should go home," said Bess with a nervous glance around.

"I don't think it's dangerous," said Mrs. Thomkins with a reassuring smile. "But it's certainly upsetting."

"What is it?" Wren felt as if she'd burst if she

didn't hear it soon.

Mrs. Thomkins leaned forward with a frown. Lines deepened from the corners of her eyes and spread to her white curls. "My newspapers have been disappearing."

Wren stiffened with disappointment while Bess sighed in relief.

Mrs. Thomkins swallowed hard and folded her hands on the table near her cup and saucer. "I receive a paper every day, but during the past three weeks some of my papers have disappeared."

Wren's face lit up. "Disappeared?"

"Yes. I called the paper boy and he said that he always delivers my paper right at my front porch and that he didn't miss any days at all. I called the police to report it, but they won't do anything. Then I talked to Amos and he said I should call you since you're good about solving mysteries."

"I'm glad you did!" Suddenly it was exciting again. "Can you tell me anything else?"

"I've been watching for the paper boy so that I could get outdoors and get my paper before it disappears, but he comes so early that sometimes I'm still asleep and miss him."

Wren rubbed her hands down her jeans. Now was the time for logic. Dad had said often that detective work took a lot of clear thinking. "Have you noticed a pattern, a particular day that your papers are missing?"

"I don't think so. This morning's paper was gone

and that's when I reached the end of my rope. I couldn't take it anymore."

"This is Thursday." Wren thoughtfully hooked her dark hair behind her ears. "Did you get a paper yesterday?"

"Yes."

"The day before?"

Mrs. Thomkins nodded.

"When was the last time you didn't get one?" Wren leaned forward in anticipation.

Mrs. Thomkins frowned in thought. "Let me think now." She was silent and the ticking of the clock on the wall behind the table sounded loud. "It was Friday!" Her face lit up. "Yes it was Friday!"

"How about Thursday of last week?"

"Yes!"

"How about the week before that?"

Mrs. Thomkins absently fingered her coffee cup as she thought. Finally she nodded. "Yes. Yes, it was Thursday and Friday of the week before that too!"

"So what does that mean?" asked Bess.

Wren puffed up with pride. "The person that steals the papers only steals them on Thursdays and Fridays."

"But why?" asked Bess.

"That's what I'd like to know," said Mrs. Thomkins.

"I'll find the answer to that," said Wren with

great confidence. "And who's been taking the papers, too."

Mrs. Thomkins smiled in relief. "Thank you, Wren. Amos said I could count on you."

"I'll have to stake out your place," said Wren.

"On a school morning?" asked Bess, her eyes wide in surprise. At Wren's frown she closed her mouth and leaned back against her chair.

Wren whipped out her tiny red notebook and the stub of pencil that she carried in her pocket. "What time does the paper boy come?"

"Between six-thirty and seven-thirty each morning."

"That's early," said Bess. "You can't be here that early, Wren."

"Oh, I wouldn't expect that, Wren." Mrs. Thomkins shook her head. "I thought maybe you could talk to the paper boy again."

"What's his name?"

"Brad Elery. He's just a boy. Fourteen, I think."

"I don't know him. Do you, Bess?"

"No."

"He must go to public school. Do you know his address?"

"No, but I have his phone number." Mrs. Thomkins walked to the counter and pulled a piece of paper from under a jar.

"I'll give him a call right now if that's all right with you." At a nod from Mrs. Thomkins, Wren quickly dialed the number. Wren's stomach tightened when a woman answered. She took a deep breath. "May I speak to Brad Elery, please."

"Just a moment." There was a pause, then a shout. "Brad. Phone. Don't stay on long. It's almost time to eat."

Wren shot a look at the clock and her heart sank. She had to get home to help with dinner.

"Hello."

"Brad, this is Wren . . . . " She hesitated. "Wren House."

"Stop fooling around. Who is this?"

"My name really is Wren House. I'd like to talk to you about your paper route."

"Is this you, Margaret?"

"No! I'm here with Mina Thomkins on Maple Street."

"Penny! It's you. Isn't it?"

"This is business. I need to find out why Mrs. Thomkins isn't getting her paper."

"Is this on the level?"

"Yes."

"About my paper route?"

"Yes. Mrs. Thomkins and her missing papers."

"I already talked to her. I told her I delivered her papers every day. It's not my fault if someone steals them."

"How do you know they're being stolen?"

"Simple. I deliver them. She doesn't get them. Someone must take them."

"But why?"

"How should I know? I'm not a detective."

"I am."

Brad was silent for several seconds. "Is this Sally?"

"I am Wren House from Lyons Street and I'm going to solve this case of the missing newspapers. But I need your help."

"You'd better not be putting me on." Brad sounded unsure of himself.

"I'm not. Tell me what time you'll deliver the paper in the morning."

"When I get there."

Wren tapped her pencil on her pad. "What time?"

"Between six-thirty and seven-thirty. Depends on when I get there."

"Can't you be more specific?"

"Why should I?"

"I want to stake out the house."

"Stake it out? You must watch a lot of TV."

"My dad's a detective and he taught me how."

"Is your dad Sam House?"

Wren swelled up with pride. "Yes! Do you know him?"

"No. But I've read about him before. He's famous."

"I know. Now, tell me what time you'll be here in the morning."

"I'll try my best to be there at seven. Does that help?"

"Yes. Thanks."

"I'll see you then."

Wren shook her head hard. "No. You won't be able to see me. I'll be hiding. I can't have you give me away."

"All right, but let me know when you find the thief."

"I will. And thanks for your help."

"You're welcome. Is this really Wren House?"

"Yes."

"That's a strange name."

"I know. My mother named me so no one would forget my name once they heard it."

"I sure won't forget it."

"Thanks again. Goodbye."

"Goodbye. Wren House . . . are you sure this isn't Penny?"

Wren sighed. "It's not. Bye." She turned back to Mrs. Thomkins and Bess. "I'll be here just before seven and hide outdoors." She could see herself sneaking around the house and hiding behind a bush or up close to the porch.

"It's still almost dark out at seven," said Bess.

Wren shrugged. This was a real case to solve, and darkness wouldn't stop her from solving it. "I'll bring a flashlight if I need to."

Bess shivered. "I wouldn't do it, Wren. It's dangerous. What if someone really mean or bad is taking the papers? You could be hurt."

"I hadn't thought of that," said Mrs. Thomkins. "Wren, I can't ask you to do it."

"As your very best friend I think I should stop you," said Bess.

Wren squared her shoulders and tried to look older. "Don't worry. I'm used to a life of danger and intrigue."

"Well, if you're sure," said Mrs. Thomkins, hiding a smile behind her hand.

"I am. Let's go, Bess. I have to get home to help with dinner. See you in the morning, Mrs Thomkins."

Wren pedaled toward home, her heart leaping and her brain whirling with plans for the morning.

5.
The House Family

Wren closed the back door carefully and leaned against it. She was late again. Smells of roast beef, cooking carrots and boiling potatoes made her stomach growl. Was it Mom or Dad in the kitchen? She took a deep breath, squared her shoulders and called, "I'm home."

"In here, Wren." It was Mom and she sounded impatient. Wren knew she worked hard all day and was too tired to fix dinner alone.

Wren walked into the kitchen. "Sorry I'm late, Mom."

Lorrene House turned from the stove, a fork in her hand. Her strawberry blond hair looked as nice as it had when she'd left home for work. A flowered apron covered her dark skirt and satiny blue blouse. Tired lines circled her blue eyes. "Neil said you might be." Lorrene pulled Wren close and kissed her cheek. Wren liked the smell of her perfume. "You must try harder to be on time, though. Being late is a bad habit to get into."

Wren relaxed. She was glad Mom wasn't angry. "I'm sorry. I forgot the time." She washed her hands at the kitchen sink. "I was talking to Mina Thomkins on Maple Street. Remember her?"

Lorrene nodded.

"Someone's taking her newspapers and she asked me to help find them."

"She did? What did she think you could do?"

Wren looked hurt. "Find them, of course." She didn't say anything about the stakeout that she had planned for the morning.

"But you're just a little girl."

"Mom . . . . I'm ten years old. I have two numbers in my age now and that means I'm practically grown up."

Lorrene laughed and shook her head. "You might seem grown up to yourself, but you're still a little girl. Enjoy being a little girl. Don't try to grow up too fast."

Wren dried her hands on the plaid towel hanging on the refrigerator door and didn't say anything. Even when she was twenty Mom would think she was still a little girl. "Is Dad in his office?"

"No. He had to meet a client and he won't be back for another half hour or so. Just in time to eat with us. Philip and Neil are both here."

Wren carried five plates to the table and set them around the way she'd learned when she was big enough to do it without breaking the plates.

While she set the table, she listened to her mom tell her about the case she'd had in court that day.

Lorrene looked up from chopping the lettuce for a salad. "How was school today?"

"All right."

"Anything new? Neil said you were putting out a newspaper."

Wren leaned against the counter and looked at a tomato. "My group has to write an article on people helping people. We don't know what to write." She told Mom about the people they'd talked to. "Nobody had a super story that we'd want to have printed."

Lorrene held her knife still. "Wren, sometimes a super story stares a person right in the face and he doesn't see it."

"What do you mean?"

"Remember how we've talked before about all the miracles from God for us? Just breathing good clean air every day into our healthy lungs is a miracle. Just being able to walk, to run and to play is a miracle. But if we take those things for granted, we don't notice them and aren't thankful to God for them." Lorrene sliced a cucumber into the salad bowl. "Look at all the stories you were told today and think about them. They are good, even great stories of people helping people. Maybe they seem unimportant to you, but think about the other side of the issue. The family that received groceries must've thought it was great to get them. The man

44

who was able to use his friend's car had to think something wonderful had happened for him. It's all in how you look at it."

Wren nodded thoughtfully. "You're right, Mom. Even if we don't see them as special, I think I'll write out all the things we heard today. Even Sean taking care of his little brothers is something great from his mom's point of view."

"That's right."

"I'll write them down and show them to the others in the group. I think I can get them to see things your way."

"I think you can, too. You're a born leader, Wren. My little Wren House, leader of the pack."

Wren laughed with delight as the words warmed her deep inside.

"Now, if you could just learn to be on time, you'd be almost perfect." Lorrene chuckled and Wren grinned sheepishly.

"I'll try harder, Mom."

"Good. It's important to be on time."

"I know." Wren watched in silence as Lorrene finished the salad.

"By the way, your piano lesson is set for Friday after school. You can stop at Mrs. Larkin's house on your way home from school and take your lesson. She'll have the books you'll need."

Every word seemed to tighten an icy band around Wren's heart. "Can we talk about this?"

"Of course. What do you want to say?"

Wren took a deep breath and tried to steady her voice. "I don't want to take piano lessons."

"I know that's what you think right now, but later you'd be sorry."

"No, I wouldn't."

Lorrene pushed the cut up vegetables into the bowl, then wiped her hands on a paper towel. "Wren, you will take piano lessons every Friday after school for the next few years." Her voice was kind but firm and Wren knew it wouldn't do any good to argue. "It's as important to develop your creative skills as it is your academic skills."

Wren sighed. "All right, Mom."

"You'll thank me some day."

Wren rolled her eyes. "I don't think so."

"You will." Lorrene drained the potatoes and set the pot on the counter. Steam rolled up and the aroma filled the kitchen. "Wren, call Philip to come mash the potatoes, please."

Wren ran to the hallway and shouted, "Philip, come mash the potatoes."

Philip leaped out of his bedroom and bounded down the hall. He was sixteen and all the girls at school thought he was good looking. They envied Wren for having him as a brother. "Potatoes, here I come!"

With a laugh, Wren stepped aside before he bowled her over. He was proud of the muscles that he'd worked so hard to get and he liked to show them off when he worked. She watched him push the masher into the steaming potatoes. She'd tried to mash them before, but she didn't have enough strength to do it without leaving lumps. She was glad Mom didn't say anything more about piano lessons.

Neil dashed into the kitchen, stopped beside his mom, and draped an arm around her shoulders. "Mmm. I'm hungry. How long before we eat?"

"Just as soon as your dad gets here. You can drain the water off the carrots and pour them into that bowl, then put a dab of butter on top."

Neil wrinkled his nose. "Carrots? Ugh."

"We can't eat corn every night," said Lorrene with a grin.

Wren turned at a sound behind her to find Dad walking into the kitchen. "Dad!" She flung herself into his strong arms and he lifted her high and hugged her until it was almost impossible to breathe. He kissed her and slid her to the floor.

He kept his hands on her shoulders as he smiled down into her upturned face. He wore a gray business suit, white shirt and a striped tie pulled loose at his neck. "Any new mysteries, Wren?"

"Mrs. Thomkins's newspapers keep disappearing and she doesn't know who takes them. I'm going to solve the case of the missing newspapers for her."

"Good for you." He turned to Lorrene, kissed her, spoke to the boys and then picked up the knife to slice the roast. "Smells delicious and looks good enough to eat. Anybody hungry?" His dark eyes twinkled as he looked around.

A few minutes later, after they'd thanked God for the food, Neil said, "Dad, do you know any great stories about people helping people?"

"I was going to ask him," said Wren.

"What's this all about?" asked Sam as he spooned carrots onto his plate.

"We're putting out a school paper," said Philip. "High school students take the articles that the other classes write and put them together to form a paper."

"And my group is writing about people helping people," said Neil.

Wren's fork clattered to her plate. "What? Your group!" Her voice rose to a screech and the others stared at her in surprise.

Sam caught Wren's arm. "Wren, what's wrong?"

"My group is writing the same thing! How will we find anything to write about? The eighth graders will take all the good ideas."

"That's right," said Neil with a smug grin.

"See?" Wren looked helplessly at Dad. "What chance do we have?"

Sam smiled from Wren to Neil and back again. "There are more than enough stories to go around. You both know a lot of people and you won't have any trouble finding different stories."

"I guess you're right," said Wren, remembering

that she and Bess had asked the Lord to help them.

Neil swallowed a drink of water, then set his glass back in place. "There's no competition, Wren. The great eighth graders naturally will have a better article than the lowly fifth graders."

"Neil," Mom and Dad said in the same warning voice. They didn't like teasing that hurt someone.

Wren took a deep breath. No way would she let Neil beat her. "Call us what you want, Neil. We'll still turn in the best article in the entire school!"

"Even if you have to make it up," said Philip with a laugh.

Wren frowned. "We wouldn't do that." But should they? It did sound like a good idea, especially if they couldn't find a truly great story. They could make up a really super article and have the best one in the first paper. A guilty feeling rose inside her and Wren quickly brushed it aside.

6.
The Stakeout

Wren dropped her bathrobe over the end of her bed and pulled back the covers. The idea of making up a story had filled her until all she could think about was doing it.

Who would ever know the difference? Who would even care?

She swallowed hard and ran her tongue over her dry bottom lip. She didn't dare answer those questions even in her own mind. She'd just go ahead and make up a story, write it in her best handwriting and hand it in.

Her stomach knotted and she turned away from her bed and stared down at the heap of dirty clothes in the corner of her room. She shivered and rubbed her hands up and down her arms. It really was getting cold. Maybe she should ask Dad to turn up the heat.

She cleared her throat. "This should be easy." With an unsteady hand she tucked her hair, still damp from her shower, behind her ears. She tugged at the neckline of her warm nightgown and pushed the long sleeves up to her elbows.

"I'm going to sit at my desk and write a story," she said in a low, tense voice. "A story that's better than the eighth graders'." But she didn't move. For some reason, she couldn't.

Down the hall the phone rang and she stood motionless. No one ever called her this late at night, but for some strange reason she knew it was going to be for her. She slipped on her robe, tied the belt and ran out the door. The boys were still watching TV with Mom and Dad in the living room. She heard Dad answer the phone. He was used to getting calls at night.

"I'm sorry, but she's already in bed," Wren heard him say into the phone.

She stood in the doorway, her heart racing. "I'm right here, Dad." Her voice was low and quivery, but he heard her.

He turned with a frown. "You're supposed to be in bed."

"I know. I heard the phone."

"It's for you." He lowered his voice. "Don't stay on long."

"I won't." Her hand shook as it closed over the phone. "Hello."

"Wren, it's me. Mrs. Thomkins."

Wren stood very still. Was she going to lose her first real job as a detective? "Hello, Mrs. Thomkins." Her voice shook and she touched her hand to her throat.

Mrs. Thomkins was silent several seconds and Wren felt as if her legs had turned to water. "Wren, I just wanted to make sure that you're going to be here in the morning."

Wren sagged in relief against the wall. Light danced in her eyes and she held back a giggle. Laughter burst from the TV and was joined with her family's chuckles. "I'll be there, Mrs. Thomkins. You can count on me."

Mrs. Thomkins sighed heavily. "I'm not feeling very well and I know I won't get up in time to guard my paper."

"Don't worry about a thing. Your papers are safe with me." Wren puffed up with pride. "I'll take care of everything."

Mrs. Thomkins laughed a frail little laugh. "Good for you, Wren. I should've known everything would be all right, but I started thinking about it and couldn't get to sleep until I knew that you'd be here. But be careful, won't you?"

"I will. 'Bye." Wren turned from the phone and met her dad's eyes.

"Who was that?" Sam asked.

"Mrs. Thomkins. She wanted to make sure that I'm still going to help her with her missing papers."

"And are you?" Lorrene asked.

Wren nodded. "Of course."

Her mom cocked an eyebrow. "Just so you don't forget your piano lesson tomorrow."

Wren wrinkled her nose. "I won't. No matter how hard I try." Wren turned to go back to her bedroom, but caught the questioning look in her dad's eyes. Suddenly she knew she couldn't just sneak out of the house in the morning.

Concern edged her voice as she asked her dad, "Could we talk in my bedroom for awhile? I need to ask you something."

Sam shot a quick look at Lorrene, then said, "Sure, Wren."

The next morning, her teeth chattering from the cold, Wren moved closer to the corner of Mrs. Thomkins's front porch. She zipped her winter jacket up to her neck, lifted the collar and hunched down into it. Street lights glowed, making Wren feel as if it were still night instead of six forty-five in the morning. Alone in the stillness she remembered the long talk she'd had with her dad about this plan for her early morning stakeout. She'd been pleased and almost surprised when he had finally agreed to it.

A brisk wind blew leaves across the quiet street. The noise startled Wren. A block away car lights stabbed the darkness and then turned the corner away from Wren's hiding place. She waited in silence. The wind chilled her to her very bones. Every tiny noise made her jump.

"Brad Elery, where are you?" The whisper sounded loud and she pressed her blue lips closed. It wouldn't do to blow her cover just because she hated to wait. Dad had told her that waiting was part of the game. She might as well get used to it.

Just then a teen-aged boy on a bike whizzed along the sidewalk, flinging rolled papers to the houses. Wren waited, every nerve tense. Instead of riding past Mrs. Thomkins's house, though, he carried the paper right to the porch. The street light shone on his dark face. He peered around and Wren stood very still. Her heart raced. Was he going to give her away?

"Wren? Wren House, come out if you're here."

She didn't move.

"I should've known someone was playing a trick on me."

In a strangled voice she whispered, "Get out of here! Do you want to give me away before I catch whoever is taking the paper?"

He laughed low in his throat and looked closer. "I had to make sure that you're real."

"I am, now get out of here."

"Come out where I can see you."

"I can't! Now, leave before it's too late." Frustration churned inside her. "You're messing up my whole plan."

"Sorry." He peered closer at the bushes hiding Wren. "Will you promise to let me know how this turns out?"

She knotted her fingers together. "I promise," she said through clenched teeth. "Now go!"

With a shrug and a low sigh he dropped the paper on the porch and rode away, whistling into the wind.

Wren glanced around, her heart in her mouth. Had she been spotted? She moved restlessly. A branch from the evergreen bush jabbed into her side. She jerked and bumped against the porch pillar. The sounds seemed to burst out and shatter the silence.

Flushing, she pulled back and stood quietly, barely breathing. Her eyes hurt from staring at the paper and the area around her.

Maybe the thief wouldn't show up this morning. Maybe there wasn't a thief. Wren frowned at the terrible thought.

"Psst. Wren? Are you here?"

She peeked around the bush, her heart racing. "Wren? Where are you?"

She slapped her hand over her mouth to hold back an angry scream. She stepped around the bush. "Tim! What are you doing here?"

Tim huddled into his jacket. "Bess called me last night and told me you'd be here."

Wren grabbed his arm and tugged. "Get out of sight, will you? Do you want to give me away?"

He ducked behind the bush with her. "Spot anything yet?" he asked in a low voice.

"You probably scared him off," she snapped.

"Sorry."

"Why did you come?"

"Bess was worried about you."

"I told her that I'd be all right."

"Well, you know Bess. She said you might need my help if someone really was stealing the papers." Tim moved restlessly. "I hope I didn't mess things up for you. I wouldn't want to do that."

She sighed heavily. "I know."

"Hold it! Look!" Tim gripped her arm and she turned her head to watch someone sneaking across the lawn. A flashlight beam bobbed across the grass and sidewalk and finally landed on the newspaper laying on the porch.

A chill ran down Wren's spine. She heard Tim suck in his breath. She locked her hands together and her brain whirled with ideas. What should she do next?

7.
A Strange Encounter

Wren held her breath and watched the flashlight beam slide up and down the porch steps and across the newspaper again. This had to be it. Her stakeout had paid off. She was glad her dad knew what she was doing.

Tim stepped closer to Wren until their arms touched and waited without speaking. Car lights stabbed a path along the street and disappeared. In the distance a siren wailed.

Just then Wren heard a strange sniffing and grunting sound coming from the front yard. She frowned and looked around, but couldn't see anything. Were they going to be discovered before solving the case?

Tim put his mouth close to Wren's ear. "What's that?"

Wren shrugged, but didn't speak for fear of being heard. A shiver ran over her.

The person walked closer to the porch, a darker

shadow in the shadows of the house. "Here, Suie. Suie, get away from that bush." It was a woman and her voice was low and tense.

Wren bit her bottom lip and peered frantically around. Suie? Who was Suie? Were they going to be seen?

Just then the grunting, sniffing sound grew louder. Wren had heard similar sounds from a bear at the zoo. Her heart plunged to her feet and she bit back a cry of panic. She felt Tim's fear and that sent a new wave of shivers down her spine. Something was just on the other side of the bush and it was going to get them any second.

Something touched her leg and she looked down. Wren opened her mouth to scream but no sound came out. A huge, ugly, four-legged creature stood there with its snout touching her. For a minute she couldn't move. Then she leaped forward with a startled cry and stopped at the bottom of the steps.

The woman cried out and almost dropped the flashlight. "Oh, my! Who's there? What's wrong?" She shot the beam at Wren and caught her in the eyes with it. "A little girl! What're you doing here?"

Wren blinked, blinded for a minute. "There's something terrible, really terrible over . . . over there!" She pointed with a trembling finger.

"It almost got us," said Tim, standing close to Wren.

The woman caught Tim in her light. "Another kid!"

The snorting, grunting sounds grew louder. Wren caught at Tim and gripped the material of his jacket sleeve.

"Suie!" cried the woman. "Come here!" She turned the light toward the strange sounds, but caught only a strange round rump in the light as it ran off into the darkness.

Just then the porch light went on, bathing Wren, Tim, and the woman in light. The door opened. Mrs. Thomkins peered out, her face pale. "What's going on out here? Wren, is that you?"

Wren shivered and wanted to dash for the safety of the house, but she stood her ground. She was a detective and she didn't run when the going got tough. "It's me. With Tim and someone . . . someone else." She didn't mention the thing that had just run away.

The woman beside Wren looked around as if she was going to run. "I just came to get my pet. I'll be going now."

"Where is your pet?" asked Tim.

"I don't know."

"I think something frightened it away," said Wren. "There was something terrible over there, but it ran away. It was just awful! Maybe it was after your pet." Wren shivered and looked in the direction the animal had gone.

"I'd better find my pet," said the woman in a stiff

voice. She looked pale in the light from the porch. She was old, but not as old as Mrs. Thomkins. Her head was covered with a battered hat and she wore a heavy plaid jacket and dark pants.

Mrs. Thomkins stepped out on the porch and pulled her warm robe tighter around her frail body. "Do you live around here?"

The woman hesitated, then nodded. "Just next door. I'm Mrs. Ruth Banner."

"I've been wanting to meet you, but you haven't been home when I've come over. I'm Mina Thomkins and these two are my friends, Wren and Tim."

Ruth Banner nodded, turned and scurried away.

"That was strange," said Wren.

"I wonder if she was going to take the paper," said Tim with a thoughtful look on his freckled face.

"I don't think so," said Mrs. Thomkins.

"Let's follow her home," said Wren. "We missed the thief. He was probably frightened off with all the noise."

Tim ran a hand over his red hair. "Wren, it could've been Mrs. Banner."

"I don't think so, either, Tim, but Dad always says not to rule out any possibilities, so I'll keep an open mind." Wren picked up the newspaper and handed it to Mrs. Thomkins. "I'll see you after my piano lesson, Mrs. Thomkins. I'm sorry I haven't solved the case yet, but I won't give up."

"Thank you. I know I can count on you." Mrs. Thomkins closed the door with a gentle click.

Wren turned to Tim, motioning toward the house next door. "Let's go."

"I'm with you, Wren." Tim grinned and they both dashed around the house to the house next door. They stopped short at the sight of the woman standing near the curb bathed in the glow from the streetlight. The sky was much lighter and traffic sounds were louder from the highway.

"Suie!" Mrs. Banner called. "Come, Suie. Where are you? Come back to me right now! You know it's not safe for you to be out here."

Wren took a deep breath and stepped into the light. "Do you need help to find your pet?"

Mrs. Banner frowned. "I don't want trouble from you kids."

"We want to help," said Tim.

"We do," said Wren.

Mrs. Banner wiped away a tear that slipped down her weathered cheek. "I can't find Suie."

"Is it your cat?" asked Tim.

Mrs. Banner pulled off her battered hat to show flattened gray hair. She ran her long fingers through her hair, set her hat back in place and sighed. "Suie's my pet."

"A cat?" asked Wren.

"No."

Tim looked around, then back at Mrs. Banner. "A dog?"

"Not exactly."

Wren narrowed her eyes suspiciously. "Just what is Suie?"

"I don't know if I should say."

Wren took a deep breath. "A bear! Is Suie a bear?"

Tim gasped.

Mrs. Banner laughed shakily. "No. Not a bear."

Wren cleared her throat. "Then what? We can't find it if we don't know what we're looking for."

Mrs. Banner shifted her weight from one foot to the other. "Suie's my pig. My pet pig and I've had her for over a year now."

Wren's mouth dropped open and stayed that way for a long time.

Tim burst out laughing. "A pig? Here in town?"

Wren finally found her voice. "A pig? A real pig?"

Mrs. Banner stepped forward. "Shh. Please, don't tell anyone. Suie's the only part of my past that I could bring from my farm. I love her. I won't give her up!"

"A pig!" whispered Wren.

"I fought to keep her from being slaughtered and I'll fight to keep her here with me."

Wren and Tim exchanged looks and they both nodded. "We'll help you find her," said Wren with a smile.

"But we'd better hurry," said Tim. "It's really light now, and we have to go to school soon."

Mrs. Banner looked frightened. "I've got to get her inside out of sight right now!"

"I'll look that way. Tim you go that way and Mrs. Banner, you walk around your house and call Suie." Wren dashed off, looking here and there for a pig. A laugh bubbled up inside her and burst out. She had come to stake out Mrs. Thomkins's place to find a newspaper thief only to chase down a runaway pig. Dad had said the detective business could be strange.

Just then Wren saw the big white pig rooting up a flower bed. "Suie, come here," called Wren just as loud as she dared. "Suie."

The pig lifted its head. Dirt fell off its snout. It was all white except for a black circle on its rump. Pink skin showed through the bristles of hair. It turned and Wren trembled. Little beady eyes stared at her and Suie snorted, blowing more dirt. A collar hung around the huge neck.

"Come, Suie." Wren's voice shook. In all of her ten years, she'd never run across a pig before.

Suie grunted and ran to her.

Wren trembled and forced herself to reach for the collar. "You have to get home, Suie. Come on." Wren closed her eyes and slipped her hand between the collar and the white bristles.

A few minutes later she walked Suie into Mrs. Banner's yard.

"Suie!" cried Mrs. Banner from where she stood near her front porch. "Oh, Suie, you're back!"

Suie snorted, tugged hard and pulled free to run to Mrs. Banner.

Wren ran after her just as Tim dashed into the yard. "We'll help you get her inside," said Wren. She opened the door and Mrs. Banner shooed Suie inside, then turned with eyes full of fear to Tim and Wren.

"You'll keep my secret, won't you?" Mrs. Banner's voice trembled and her face was gray.

"I will," said Tim.

"Me, too," said Wren.

"Thank you! Suie thanks you, too. She wouldn't know how to live without me. I've had her since she was two days old. I fed her with an eye dropper and then with a baby bottle until she could eat on her own. She's all the family I have left." Her voice broke and she blinked back tears. "Thank you again. And please, please, don't breathe a word to anyone about her, not even to your friend Mrs. Thomkins."

"We promise," said Wren, and Tim nodded.

"Could we come sometime and play with her?" asked Tim.

Wren stared at him in surprise. Just how did you play with a pig?

"I'd like you to come." Mrs. Banner pulled off her hat and wrinkled the brim. "I get lonely since I moved to town and away from my friends."

"We'll come soon," said Wren. She hated for anyone to be lonely. "We have to go now so we can get to school."

After the door closed behind Mrs. Banner, Wren turned to Tim. "Think what Paula Gantz would do with this news."

Tim rolled his eyes. "This is one secret we'll never let her know."

Wren nodded and ran to where she'd left her bike.

"Let me know when you're going to stake out Mrs. Thomkins's place again," said Tim. "I want to help you crack this case."

"Thanks, Tim. It would be better to have you with me." Wren picked up her bike. "Do you still think it could've been Mrs. Banner?"

Tim narrowed his eyes thoughtfully. "I don't know. She's a nice lady and not the type to steal papers. But we can't let our emotions rule."

"You're right. Everyone is suspect. I hope it's not Mrs. Banner." Wren wheeled her bike to the sidewalk. "I hope it's some stranger that we don't care about."

"Why would someone steal papers?"

"Someone who needs them."

Tim tipped his head. "If we knew why someone needed the papers, then we'd know who took them."

Wren nodded. "You're probably right. Why

would someone need only Thursday and Friday papers?"

"And since he didn't get today's paper, will he come take tomorrow's?"

Wren gasped. "Maybe so! I think we'd better stake the place out again in the morning."

"I'll be here."

"At six-thirty. In the morning." Wren's mind whirled as she pedaled toward home to change into school clothes.

Alone in the shadows across the street, Sam House watched his daughter. He and Lorrene had talked long about this plan of Wren's and Sam had explained why he'd agreed to it. Now he kept watch from a close place. Ready to help Wren if necessary, he would remain silently hidden as long as she was safe. Sam knew that her desire for independence was mixed with her willingness to help her friends—and her eagerness to be a detective. Pride in her, as well as her courage and honesty with him, had led him to his own wintery stakeout.

The commotion across the street made him start forward, but he quickly realized that Wren was not in danger. He watched the kids and neighbor lady from his hiding place, chuckling softly when he saw Wren leading a pig by the collar. Although he knew the pig could not stay, he would give her a few days to work out the problem.

He smiled as he thought about the two ten-year-olds across the street, and watched as Wren and Tim rode away on their bikes. Satisfied that Wren was all right, Sam quietly followed her home.

8.
The Story

Study time at school was agony for Wren as she gripped her pencil tighter and closed her eyes in thought. This had to be the very best story in the whole school. She would not let Neil or the eighth graders turn in a better story.

Miss Brewster had said it had to be a true story. Wren tapped her lined paper with her pencil lead.

An icy band tightened around Wren's heart and a real struggle filled her heart. Was it right to hand in a made-up story?

"I don't care," she muttered. "I'm going to do it anyway."

Tears stung the backs of her eyes, but she forced them away as she bent once again over her story and wrote another sentence. She added part of a true story that she'd heard so that if Miss Brewster asked she could say it was true. Wren moved restlessly, but kept on writing. Her hand ached from holding the pencil so tightly. When she was finished, she asked for permission to hand the story to Bess to read. If Bess read it and didn't find it boring, then Wren would know it was good.

"What's this?" asked Bess.

"For the school paper. I didn't think you'd care if I went ahead and wrote it. If you know a way to make it better, tell me. If you like it the way it is, show it to Tim. He can show it to Sean and Paula."

Bess looked closely at Wren. "What's wrong, Wren?"

Wren straightened stiffly. "Did I say anything was wrong?"

"No, but you look funny."

"Just read the story, Bess, and leave me alone!" Wren flung herself back into her seat and folded her arms across her thin chest. Why couldn't Bess be quiet when she should?

Miss Brewster walked back to Wren. "Is something wrong?" she asked softly.

Wren's face was like a dark thundercloud. "Nothing's wrong!"

Miss Brewster squeezed Wren's shoulder. "You know I'm here to help if you want to talk."

Wren locked her mouth shut and stared straight ahead until finally Miss Brewster walked away, leaving a faint trail of perfume that stung Wren's nose.

Several minutes later Bess passed the story to Tim. She glanced at Wren and smiled, nodding to let Wren know she liked the story. Wren tried to smile back, but her lips were frozen in a straight line and wouldn't move. She saw the puzzled expression on Bess's face and then a hurt look. Finally Bess turned back to the work on her desk and Wren lifted her reading book to hide behind it.

After school Tim stopped her on the sidewalk. "I want to talk about the story, Wren."

She lifted her chin. "I don't have time, Tim. I have piano lessons. Remember?"

"I remember, but I want to know where you got the story."

She stiffened. "What do you mean?"

"I want to know who told you that story."

"Didn't you like it?"

He pushed his hands into his jacket pockets and hunched against the chilly wind. "Sure. I liked it. A lot. Where did you get it?"

"What does it matter?"

"I just wondered."

"I've got to go, Tim. We'll talk later."

Tim frowned. "What's the matter with you, Wren?"

"Nothing!"

"You're acting funny."

Wren pushed her face close to his. "I don't want to take piano lessons. Isn't that reason enough to act this way?"

70

Tim shrugged. "I guess. But it seems like more than that."

"What could it be?"

"Maybe the case you're working on."

She struggled through the dark cloud of guilt and managed a smile. "I should have the case solved by tomorrow at this time."

"Is it all right if I do the stakeout with you?"

"Of course. Why wouldn't it be?"

"I don't know. You're acting so funny that I thought maybe you didn't want me around. You know . . . the way you used to feel."

She flushed painfully. Once she'd hated Tim Avery and didn't want to talk to him or have him talk to her. "We're friends now. You know that."

He smiled and nodded. "Good. I was afraid you hated me again."

"I don't."

"See you in the morning outside Mrs. Thomkins's house."

She nodded and watched him ride away. She turned to head for home only to find Paula Gantz just a foot away. Wren scowled. "Are you spying on me again?"

Paula shrugged. "So, what if I am?"

"I don't have time for this. I have a piano lesson in just a few minues."

Paula gripped Wren's arm. "You made that story up, didn't you?"

Wren's legs almost buckled. Her head spun.

"What do you mean?" she finally asked in a hoarse voice.

"You know what I mean. I should go tell Miss Brewster, but I won't. It was a good story and I think it'll be the best in the whole school."

Wren swallowed hard.

Paula grinned wickedly. "I didn't know a Christian would do such a thing."

Wren still couldn't believe she'd done it. "Where is the story?"

Paula laughed as if she knew a good joke. "I handed it in, of course."

Wren's dark brows shot to her bangs. "You what?"

"Isn't that what you were going to do?"

"I guess, but not yet."

"It's in and Miss Brewster said she was glad for it. She thinks it's a true story. She wouldn't suspect that you would ever write a lie."

Wren gasped, jerked free and ran all the way to Mrs. Larkin's house. Paula's words rang in her ears and she couldn't get rid of them.

Wren stopped just outside Mrs. Larkin's front door and sucked in air until she could breathe again. The wind blew leaves down the sidewalk and across the lawns. A car drove past. Down the street a dog barked.

Wren bit her bottom lip with sharp, white teeth. How could she let everyone think that story was the truth? She'd given her life to Jesus when she was

72

only five years old and she'd always tried to live the way He wanted her to. What had made her do such a terrible thing? And what was she going to do about it?

Before she could sort it out, the door opened and Mrs. Larkin stood there smiling. She was about fifty years old with short, light brown hair and blue eyes that sparkled with excitement.

"Come in, Wren. I'm glad you're on time. Some of my students don't think it's necessary." Mrs. Larkin held the door wide and Wren walked inside.

The room was cozy and warm. A baby grand piano filled one end of the room. Pictures of students hung on the wall in back of the piano. A fire crackled in a brick fireplace on another wall. Mrs. Larkin took Wren's jacket and hung it on an oak halltree near the door.

"I'm so glad you are going to take piano, Wren. Music is important to all of us, and I know especially to you. You have a beautiful singing voice. I always enjoy hearing you."

"Thank you." Wren stood awkwardly in the middle of the room and didn't know what to say or do. How could she tell Mrs. Larkin that she hated being here when Mrs. Larkin was being so nice?

"Let's go to the piano, Wren. It's going to be a pleasure to teach you since you have such a great love for music."

Wren shot a look at the door to see if she could run for it. But she knew Mom would never let her get by with that, so she followed Mrs. Larkin across the soft carpet to the piano. She sat on the bench and looked down at the rows of black and white keys. Never in a million years could she learn to play all those keys.

"Here's your first book, Wren. You'll have this one and *Introduction to Finger Power*. Practicing diligently every day is the key to being a good pianist."

Wren's mind wandered as Mrs. Larkin talked. When it was time to actually play the first little song, Wren fumbled and felt as if all her fingers belonged to someone else. Her brain couldn't make them work at all. Finally the half hour was up and Wren slipped on her jacket, clutched the dreaded books to her chest and ran out the door.

At home she ignored Neil's teasing about taking piano lessons, flung her books on her bed, changed into jeans and a sweater, then rode her bike over to Mrs. Thomkins's. But even that didn't lift the cloud of gloom that surrounded her.

Mrs. Thomkins handed her a glass of water. "You look tired, Wren. I'm sorry for making you get up so early this morning."

"That's all right, Mrs. Thomkins."

"And all for nothing." Mrs. Thomkins sank down on a kitchen chair. "What will you do next?"

Wren wiped the back of her hand across her mouth. "I'll stake out your place in the morning."

"Saturday? But my Saturday paper has never

been taken."

Wren leaned back in her chair. "Maybe since today's paper wasn't, the thief might take tomorrow's."

Mrs. Thomkins nodded. "You've got a good head on your shoulders, Wren. I'm thankful that you're helping me. You are one of God's helpers all right."

Wren ducked her head to hide her sudden flush. She didn't want to think about God right now, not after what she'd done at school.

Mrs. Thomkins fingered the spoon that lay next to her coffee cup. "I will try my best to wake up in the morning and keep watch with you."

"You don't have to do that. Tim said he'd come over."

"That's nice of him."

"He likes doing detective work as much as I do." Wren moved uneasily. For the first time ever the words didn't zip through her and send her leaping and shouting. Could it be that she didn't want to be a detective any longer?

Later she walked her bike slowly down the sidewalk. A cool wind whipped her brown hair into a mess, but she didn't notice.

Something was wrong with her, very wrong. Maybe she'd go through her whole life sad and miserable. Maybe she'd decide that she wanted to be a musician instead of a detective. A tear slipped down her cheek and she let it fall.

9.
Jason

Wren reached to open her back door. She had managed to put the story behind her and now her head was full of ways to find the person who was stealing Mrs. Thomkins's papers.

"Hey, Wren!"

She turned to see Bess run across the yards toward her. Bess looked very excited.

"Wren, Mom says we can go with her to meet the Cole family. She has some business papers to take to them."

Wren frowned, a blank look on her face.

"You remember. Mom sold them a house in the country. They have the boy named Jason who has something wrong with him." Bess waited, watching Wren expectantly. "You thought there might be a mystery."

"Oh, yes! I remember now. What about it?"

"We're going to see them and Mom said you might like going with us to meet the family. They're new and they need friends. They live on a real farm."

"I don't know, Bess."

"What? That's not like you at all, Wren House! Do you want to go with us, or not?"

"Oh, I guess so, but I'll have to ask Mom."

"My mom already talked to your mom and it's all set. Let's go." Bess took a step forward, stopped and thumped her chest. "And I get to sell them a subscription to our school paper."

Wren shrugged, and a sad feeling filled her. She didn't want to think about the school paper, not now, not until she could forget what she'd done.

Several minutes later Grace Talbot turned into the long drive that led to the Cole farm. A movement in the trees caught Wren's attention. She peered through the back car window and as she did, she saw Ruth Banner step from behind a tree. Wren blinked and looked again only to find that Mrs. Banner had disappeared. Wren frowned. Had she been seeing things or had she really seen Mrs. Banner?

"What's wrong, Wren?" asked Bess.

"Did you just see a woman in those trees?" Wren pointed toward them.

"I wasn't looking," said Bess. "You're not going to find a mystery, are you, Wren? I would really be embarrassed if you did."

"Oh, Bess!" Wren slipped out of the car and looked back down the long drive. She felt like going home. Sometimes Bess made her very angry.

"Come, girls," Grace Talbot called over her slender shoulder as she walked toward the large white house. Bess had the same blond hair and blue eyes as her mother.

Wren hung back, but Bess caught her arm and pulled her forward.

Inside the house Grace introduced the girls to Simon and Wanda Cole and their two sons, Levi and Jason. Wren watched Jason closely, but he looked fine to her.

"Levi, take the girls to the barn and show them the horses," said Wanda Cole with a smile.

Levi nodded his curly brown head and mischief sparkled in his brown eyes. "I have a horse of my own. Jason's only eight so he has a pony. I'm ten."

"So are we," said Bess as she followed Levi out the door.

Wren walked beside Jason. "What's your pony's name, Jason?"

Jason ducked his head without speaking.

Levi looked over his shoulder at Wren. "Jason can't talk right now. He doesn't talk at all."

"Why not?" asked Bess.

Wren saw Jason's face turn brick red and she knew he didn't want to be discussed.

Levi stopped at the barn door. "The doctor said that Jason got so frightened about the fire that his vocal chords closed. The doctor said that one of these days they'll start to work again and he'll be able to talk again. Right, Jason?"

Jason nodded.

"What fire?" asked Wren.

"Our house burned down and Jason was trapped inside. He would've died, but Dad got him out just in time."

"What a story!" cried Bess. "Wren, that's what we should write for our paper."

Wren locked her suddenly icy hands behind her back.

"What paper?" asked Levi.

Bess explained while Jason pushed open the barn door and led the way inside to the horses in the stalls. He tugged on Wren's sleeve and pointed at a black pony with a white circle around its left eye. He tapped his chest and nodded his head.

"Your pony," said Wren and Jason nodded harder. "He's cute. Will he bite me if I pet him?"

Jason shook his head, opened the stall door and led the way inside. Down the aisle a horse nickered and another answered. A tiger cat mewed from the top of a bale of hay. At the stall door Levi and Bess stopped, but continued to talk about Jason.

Wren frowned at Bess, but she looked away with a quick flick of her head.

Jason wrapped his arms around the pony's neck and pushed his face into the dusty hair. When he turned Wren saw tears in his eyes.

"Want to take me outdoors and show me around?" she asked him with a smile.

He nodded and she could tell he was glad to get away from Levi and Bess.

"Let's walk to those trees," said Wren, pointing. "I am sure I saw someone walking there, someone that I know from town."

Jason shrugged, but led the way at a full run, his thin legs pumping up and down. Wren hesitated and then followed him. She wanted to do something to help him, something that would open up his throat so he could speak again. She couldn't imagine how it would be if she couldn't talk. She started to pray silently for him, then stopped abruptly. How could she talk to God after what she'd done today?

Just then Jason stopped and turned to wait for her. He pointed up in a tree and she saw big, red apples. He pretended to pick one and bite into it.

"Do you want an apple, Jason?"

He nodded.

She jumped up and grabbed the tip of a branch, bent it low and picked an apple. She handed it to him and he jabbed a finger at her.

"You want me to have one, too?" she asked and he nodded again. She jumped for the branch again, bent it low and picked another apple. She bit into it with a loud crunch and juice squirted onto her face and hand. The apple was white inside and dark red on the outside. "It's delicious, Jason, the most delicious apple I've ever eaten. I didn't know there were still apples on the trees."

He nodded and took another bite.

Just then a pig pushed through the underbrush and stopped at Jason's side. He looked down at the pig in surprise. It was a huge white pig with a black circle on its rump. Wren looked closer. The pig looked just like Mrs. Banner's pet pig.

"Suie?" Wren said.

The pig snorted, reached out and took the apple from Jason's hand and ate it in one chomp. It rooted against Jason's hand for more.

Jason giggled.

Wren's mouth dropped open as she stared at Jason.

His eyes grew big and round and he pointed to his mouth.

"You laughed, Jason! You did!"

He nodded and opened his mouth to try again, but no sound came out. He tried harder, but still no sound. Giant tears filled his eyes.

Wren patted his shoulder. "Don't cry, Jason. One sound came out and another one will too. Relax. Don't worry about it. You'll be able to laugh and talk before you know it."

Jason knuckled away his tears and circled the pig's neck with both his thin arms.

Wren gingerly touched the pig's ear. "How'd you get here, Suie?"

"I brought her," said Ruth Banner, stepping

around a tree.

"Mrs. Banner!" Wren stared at her in surprise. "I thought I saw you when we drove in. What're you doing here?"

Mrs. Banner twisted her scarf around her hand and bit her lower lip. "I brought Suie out to see the old place."

"The old place?"

"This was my farm. It was supposed to be my farm until I died!" Anger flashed in her eyes. "But it was sold and I was forced to move to town. Me and Suie." She slapped her leg. "Come, Suie. We must get back to town before someone else sees us."

Suie didn't move. She just stood still and let Jason hug her.

Wren smiled at the boy and the pig. "Jason, this is Mrs. Banner. I met her in town. Mrs. Banner, this is Jason. Suie made him giggle."

"Can't he talk?"

"No. But he'll be able to soon. He giggled." Wren smiled at Jason and he smiled a hesitant little smile.

Mrs. Banner stepped up to Suie. "Come, Suie. We're going home. I mean, back to town where we live now. Come on! I've got to get you loaded in my pickup."

Suie grunted, but didn't move.

"She likes you, Jason," said Wren. She turned to Mrs. Banner. "Maybe you could bring Suie here again to visit with Jason."

"Why should I?"

"It might help Jason."

Mrs. Banner pushed her hands deep into the pockets of her big coat. "I suppose we could come back."

Jason looked up hopefully.

"Tomorrow?" asked Wren. For some reason it was very important to her to help Jason.

Mrs. Banner hesitated and finally nodded. "Tomorrow. In the morning about ten o'clock."

"Jason will come right out here in the trees and meet you. Won't you, Jason?"

Jason nodded hard.

"Let's help Mrs. Banner get Suie to her pickup."

"I parked it just off the road over there." Mrs. Banner jabbed a thumb over her shoulder. "I didn't want to be spotted in case I got kicked off my own place."

"If you didn't want to sell, why did you?" asked Wren as they walked Suie to the pickup.

"I didn't! Four years ago when my husband died, my son said I should sell the place to Laurence Tooker with the understanding that I could live here all the rest of my days. I agreed because he wanted to farm it. A few months ago, though, he decided to sell it and he said I'd have to move when it was sold. He wouldn't keep his promise. My son Cliff lives in England and he couldn't do anything for me, so I moved to town to the house on Maple that Rob had bought as a rental fifteen years ago."

Mrs. Banner leaned weakly against the pickup. "Things never seem to work out the way you want."

"I'm sorry," said Wren.

"You're a nice girl. I'm glad you helped me this morning and again now with Suie. She's all I've got." Mrs. Banner walked around to the back of the pickup where she had a board ramp propped against the back of the pickup. "Up you go, Suie."

Suie hesitated long enough to give Jason a chance to hug her one last chance, then she ran up the ramp and scrambled noisily into the back of the pickup. She rooted around a bit and lay down in a corner in a pile of straw.

Wren helped Mrs. Banner and Jason load the ramp, close the tailgate and lock the door of the cab.

"I'll see you in the morning, Jason," Mrs. Banner said with a smile.

Jason nodded, his eyes wide and serious.

"Goodbye, Wren. Stop and see me soon."

"I will, Mrs. Banner." Wren and Jason stepped back, watching as Mrs. Banner drove away with a clatter. "We better get back to the house before your family thinks we disappeared."

Jason nodded and took a step forward. Suddenly he stopped, turned to Wren and hugged her as tightly as he could.

She looked at him in surprise, then hugged him

84

back. "You'll talk soon, Jason," she whispered. "You will!"

He looked up with wide eyes and finally nodded.

She laughed, caught his hand in hers and ran to the house.

10.
The Mystery Solved

Wren huddled up against the porch with Tim beside her. They were hidden behind a bush that cut off most of the wind, but Wren's feet ached with cold and she wished she'd put on two pairs of socks.

"Did you tell the paper boy that you'd be here again today, Wren?" Tim's whisper exploded into the silence.

"Not so loud!" Wren moved away from a pointed branch. "I didn't tell him. I thought it might be better if no one knew except Mrs. Thomkins, my dad and us."

"Good thinking."

"A good detective can't be too careful." She pulled her cap lower over her ears. "I think we'd better be quiet. We don't want anyone to hear us."

Suddenly Tim grabbed her arm. "Look!" he hissed close to her ear.

She turned to see a flashlight beam bobbing along just as it had yesterday. Was Mrs. Banner out walking her pig again? Wren smiled as she thought about Jason and Suie together. She'd wanted to tell his family that he'd giggled, but Jason had stopped her with a tug on her sleeve and a shake of his head. It had been very hard to keep the exciting news a secret, but she'd bit her tongue and kept quiet. Later this morning Jason would have Suie to play with again. Maybe he would giggle again, or even speak.

The flashlight shone up onto the porch and Wren stood very still as she waited. Shivers ran down her spine. The paper boy hadn't arrived yet.

The light flashed away and disappeared. Wren stared into the shadows after the person. Should she follow or should she guard the house and paper? She didn't dare ask Tim what he thought in case the person with the flashlight might hear.

Just then the paper boy pedaled into sight. He flung the paper to the porch and it crashed against the door. He kept on riding and was soon out of sight.

Suddenly the beam of light shone on the paper. Wren held her breath. Butterflies fluttered in her stomach. She wanted to cry out, but she kept her mouth closed. She could feel Tim's excitement and she knew he was forcing himself to stay in place, too.

Someone walked up the steps, bent and picked up the paper.

"Get him, Tim!" cried Wren. She ran to the steps while Tim jumped up on the porch from where he stood.

The intruder threw up his arms. "Don't hurt me!"

Wren stopped short at the sound of a woman's voice. "Mrs. Banner! It *is* you!"

"Wren?" Mrs. Banner flicked the light toward Wren. "What're you doing here? You frightened me."

"Mrs. Banner. I knew it," said Tim.

Wren pointed at the paper in Mrs. Banner's hand. "Have you been taking papers from Mrs. Thomkins?"

Mrs. Banner groaned as she handed the paper to Wren. "I know it was wrong, but I had to have something for bedding for Suie. I intended to pay Mrs. Thomkins for them as soon as I could without telling about Suie."

"Where's Suie now?" asked Tim.

"I left her in the house. I didn't want her to get away from me like she did yesterday."

Wren groaned. "We'll have to tell Mrs. Thomkins."

Mrs. Banner clutched Wren's hand. "You can't tell her about Suie. She'd turn me in. A pig's not allowed in town." Her voice broke. "Please, don't tell her about Suie."

Wren sagged against the door. What should she do?

"Just tell her I took the papers and that I'll pay for them. She doesn't need to know why I took them."

"She's right," said Tim.

Wren finally nodded. "All right."

"I'll tell her that I'm sorry."

Just then the porch light clicked on and Mrs. Thomkins opened the door. "Wren?"

"It's all right, Mrs. Thomkins. Everything's under control."

Mrs. Thomkins glanced at the three. "Hi, Tim. Hello, Mrs. Banner. Out for a walk again so early?"

Mrs. Banner cleared her throat and moved from one foot to the other. "Mrs. Thomkins, I'm sorry for causing you distress. I didn't mean to."

Mrs. Thomkins frowned as she pulled her robe tighter. "What do you mean? Wren? What is she talking about?"

"Let's go inside," said Tim. "We don't want you to catch cold."

Mrs. Thomkins hesitated a moment, then stepped aside and let them enter. She looked at them with a puzzled frown. "What's going on, Wren?"

Wren pulled off her warm cap and her hair spiked out. "Mrs. Banner is very sorry about it, Mrs. Thomkins."

"About what?"

"I took your papers." Mrs. Banner held out a gloved hand. "I needed them badly and I plan to pay you for them. I'm very sorry."

"You took my papers? But why?"

"I needed them."

"For what?"

"Something personal."

"She won't do it again," said Wren. "And she will pay you for them."

"I will."

"Why didn't you just come to my door and ask for papers?" asked Mrs. Thomkins.

"I didn't know you and I was afraid. I'm new in town." Mrs Banner curled her hat brim between both hands. Her wrinkled neck and face were red and she looked like she was going to cry.

Mrs. Thomkins shook her head. "I don't understand this at all."

"Could I explain another time?" asked Wren.

"I suppose so." Mrs. Thomkins twisted the belt of her robe around her hand. "I suppose I'll have to be satisfied in knowing the case is solved." She slipped an arm around Wren. "Thank you, Wren. I'm glad Amos told me to call you. It didn't take you long at all to get to the bottom of this."

"She's a good detective," said Tim proudly.

"And a good friend," said Mrs. Banner, wiping a tear from her cheek.

"Yes," said Mrs. Thomkins.

Wren managed a smile as she held the paper out

to Mrs. Thomkins. "Do you have old papers that you don't need that Tim and I can have?"

"Old papers?"

Wren nodded.

"Yes, I do. I was saving them for a paper drive, but you can have as many as you want." Mrs. Thomkins led the way to a closet that held a neat stack of newspapers. "I don't suppose you'll tell me why you need them."

"I'm sorry," said Wren. "I can't but I promise to tell you as soon as I can."

"This is making me very curious." Mrs. Thomkins chuckled. "But I suppose I can be patient and wait for you to confide in me."

"Thanks."

Wren and Tim both picked up a bundle, said goodbye and walked out with Mrs. Banner.

"Tell us where you want them," said Wren.

"In my kitchen will be fine."

"I can bring more for you later today if you need them," said Tim.

"You're nice kids and I'm thankful for your help. So is Suie."

As they entered the house, Wren wrinkled her nose against the terrible smell. Mrs. Banner didn't seem to notice the odor. They dropped the papers on the kitchen floor in a pile.

"Do you want me to go with you today when you take Suie for a walk on your farm?" asked Wren.

"I'd like that." Mrs. Banner turned to Tim.

"Would you like to come with us?"

"I'll have to ask Adam."

"He'll let you," said Wren. She knew Adam Landon usually let Tim do almost anything he wanted.

Just then Suie ran in, grunting loudly. She dodged a chair and nudged Mrs. Banner.

Mrs. Banner laughed and patted Suie's head. "She's hungry."

"We'll leave and let you feed her," said Wren. "I'll see you after while."

A few minutes later they stood at their bikes and looked at each other. The sky was light and the wind had died down.

"A pet pig." Wren giggled.

"In the house." Tim tipped back his red head and laughed.

"What a smell!"

"Case closed," said Tim with a grin.

Wren nodded. For some reason she couldn't leap up and shout with glee.

"What's wrong?"

"I don't know." But she did know. It was because of the story that she'd written and Paula had handed in. It was always in the back of her mind, ruining her pleasure in things.

Tim walked his bike beside Wren. "I wish you'd tell me what's wrong."

"I can't."

"Why not?"

"It's too terrible."

Tim stopped and studied Wren closely. "Is it your family?"

"My family? No."

"I guess I always think having a mom who drinks is the only real terrible trouble."

"How is your mom?"

"She's still in for treatment. I went to see her a few days ago and she said she knows once she's out that she'll never drink again."

"Do you believe her?"

Tim shrugged. "I'm trying to."

"What does Adam think?"

"He says we should pray for her every day and that we should encourage her to be strong."

"That's good."

Tim inched his toe along the crack in the sidewalk. "She's afraid that I'll want to live with Adam forever, but I told her that I'm moving back with her once she's out."

Wren smiled. "You're nice, Tim."

He flushed. "Thanks."

"I'm glad we're friends."

"Me, too." He straddled his bike. "I guess I'd better go. I'll call you if I can go with you and Mrs. Banner later."

Wren nodded. As she watched Tim ride away, she wanted to call him back and pour out her terrible story, but she snapped her mouth closed and rode for home.

11.
Wren's Decision

Wren walked listlessly to her bedroom and sank onto the edge of the bed. She'd just come from telling Bess about her adventure. Bess had been impressed. Wren sighed. Why wasn't she feeling good now that her case was solved? Would she feel this way forever? Once she'd been happy and carefree, but now she was sad and depressed.

"Maybe I'm just tired." But she knew that wasn't true.

Her dad stuck his head in her doorway. He'd already shaved and he wore a light blue tee shirt and faded jeans. "Hi, Wren. I'm making French toast for breakfast. Want some?"

"Sure, Dad."

"Why the long face?"

"Nothing."

Sam sat down beside her. "Don't tell your old dad it's nothing. I know you, Wren."

She sighed. "I guess you do."

"So?"

She plucked at her bedspread. "I did something bad."

He was quiet a long time. "Yes, Wren?"

She nodded, unable to lift her head and unwilling to see the hurt in his eyes.

"What are you going to do about it?"

"I don't know."

"Did you pray?"

"I can't, Dad." She lifted an anguished face to him.

He touched her cheek with the tip of his finger. "That bad, huh?"

"Yes."

He took her hand in his. "Let me tell you something, honey. You belong to God. He is your heavenly Father. He loves you. He doesn't want you to do bad things, but if you do, He says that you should tell Him you're sorry and ask Him to forgive you. He will immediately forgive you and He'll even forget that you did wrong."

Wren thought about that a long time. "I am sorry for what I did."

"Can you make it right?"

"I could, but I'm not going to."

"Oh, Wren! Now, there's where you'll really get into trouble. If you can make it right, then you must."

"I just can't, Dad!"

"Can't? Or won't?"

She twisted her toe in the carpet. "Both, I guess."

Tears welled up in Wren's eyes as he rubbed his thumb over the back of her hand. "Let's pray that God will give you the courage to do it." He bent his head over hers.

"Heavenly Father, thank you for my precious Wren. Right now in Jesus' name I ask that your strength and your courage will help her make this wrong right. Bless her and make her a blessing to others. We love you, Father. Amen."

Wren blinked back the tears. While her dad had prayed, she'd silently told God that she was very sorry for turning in the made-up story and had asked Him to forgive her. She knew He had and her heart burst with love.

She flung her arms around her dad. "I love you, Dad. You always know how to help me most."

He grinned and kissed her cheek. "That's what dads are for."

"And you're the best."

"Thank you." He cupped her face in his large hands. "Wren, you know that I love you, don't you?"

"Yes."

"But as much as I love you, your heavenly Father loves you even more. He wants the very best for you all the time."

"I love Him, too, Dad."

"I know you do." He kissed her again. "Let's go

have breakfast."

Wren caught his hand and walked to the kitchen with him, feeling happy again. She would take the story back and she would apologize to Miss Brewster for trying to pass it off as a true happening. Everything would be all right.

Neil turned from the refrigerator. "Wren, I have the best story for our paper in the whole world!"

"That's good."

"I'd let you read it, but I don't want to make you feel bad." He chuckled and before she knew what she was doing, Wren lifted her chin. "I happen to have a good story, too." Her stomach tightened. What was she saying?

"I bet." Neil punched her playfully and laughed. "What kind of story would a little fifth grader find? Probably a cute, baby story."

"It is not!" She struggled with her temper. "It's a great story and you'll think so, too, when you read it."

"Then let me read it now."

"No way!"

"Don't fight, kids," said Sam as he took the eggs from the refrigerator.

Neil grinned at Wren and she turned away before she really got mad and yelled at him.

She stood at the sink and watched a bird outside the window until her anger was gone. She pressed her lips tightly together. No way could she take back the story from Miss Brewster now. Neil had forced her to let it stay turned in. A great sadness filled her again, but she ignored it. Neil would not turn in a better story!

"Ready for French toast, Wren?" asked Sam.

She turned, her face pale and her eyes haunted. "I'm not hungry, Dad. I'll just have a glass of juice."

"Are you sure?"

Wren nodded.

"I'll eat her share," said Neil.

Wren glared at him, drank her juice and marched out of the house. The talk with Dad in her bedroom played over in her mind and she cried out in pain.

"I can't do it," she whispered as she reached for her bike. "I can't take back the story."

"Talking to yourself, Bird House?"

Wren looked up to find Paula standing a few feet away. "What do you want?" Wren demanded.

"I'm selling subscriptions to the school paper. Want to buy one? Or maybe two so you can see your story in print?" Paula laughed as if she'd told a good joke.

"Leave me alone, Paula."

"Why? Didn't you sell any subscriptions?"

Wren frowned. She'd forgotten about it. "No, I haven't."

Paula puffed up with pride. "I've sold twenty already."

"Twenty!"

"I bet I sell the most in the whole school. Why

haven't you sold any?"

"I've been busy," Wren said stiffly.

"Being a detective, I bet."

Wren's jaw tightened. "That's right. And I solved my case this morning."

Paula flung her arms wide. "The Case of the Missing Newspapers."

Wren doubled her fists at her sides. "How did you know?"

"Bess told me."

"Bess! How could she do such a terrible thing?"

Paula shrugged. "Easily. I just walked up to her door a few minutes ago and she told me."

Wren's eyes darkened with anger. "She'll be sorry for that!"

"Was it a secret?"

"It was my business! And I don't want everyone in Jordan knowing my business!"

"Bird House is getting mean now." Paula pretended to be frightened. "We better all watch out."

"Oh, stop it! Just leave me alone!" Even as the words left her mouth Wren couldn't believe she'd said them. She usually didn't scream with anger even at Paula Gantz.

Paula's eyes widened. "What did I do to make you so mad?"

Wren picked up her bike. "Get away from me. I have important things to do."

"Like making up another story for the school paper?"

Wren gripped her handlebars until her knuckles turned white. A raging fire burned inside her as she pedaled furiously down the sidewalk.

12.
Another Decision

Wren sank low at her desk and tried to listen as Miss Brewster talked about the name for the school paper. Right now Wren didn't want to hear about the paper. She wanted to go home, crawl into bed, and cover up her head to hide from everyone, even herself.

Paula waved her arm high in the air.

"Yes, Paula."

"Miss Brewster, I think we should name the paper *NewsTime* because it's time for the news when anyone reads it."

Everyone groaned. Wren didn't move or groan.

"Paula, all the names have been turned in and the staff is deciding on the name now. You should've submitted the name you liked last Friday."

"I didn't think of it before," said Paula with a pout.

Wren traced a scratch across her desk.

Miss Brewster took a deep breath. "Let's change

101

the subject, shall we? Let's talk about subscriptions for the paper. How many do we have now, Peggy?"

Peggy walked to the folder where she kept the report, looked around to make sure everyone was watching her, and opened the folder as if it were made of delicate, handblown glass. She peered down at her writing. With a flip of her light brown hair she faced the class. "So far this class has sold seventy-three subscriptions."

"Seventy-three." Miss Brewster smiled at Peggy and motioned for her to be seated again. "Class, you've worked very hard and I'm proud of you. I would like to see you get more subscriptions in the next three days. I don't know how many the other classes have, but I know we'll have to do better than seventy-three."

Wren tried to think of people she could ask, but she couldn't think of anyone. Neil had already asked Mom and Dad and all their friends.

Several minutes later Miss Brewster stopped at Wren's desk. "I read your story again over the weekend, Wren."

Wren froze. "Oh?"

"It is a beautiful story. I thought about reading it before the class, but I felt it would be more enjoyable for them to read it for themselves in our paper."

Wren nodded. What could she say? A painful knot tightened in her stomach. She glanced away from Miss Brewster and caught the smug, knowing look on Paula's face. Wren wanted to disappear in a puff of smoke, but she sat very still and blinked away scalding tears. Never in her life had she deliberately disobeyed God.

Would she ever be able to talk with her heavenly Father again?

She ducked her head and tried to sink out of sight.

At the end of the day an assembly was called and all the classes gathered in the multipurpose room. Wren's stomach fluttered and her hands felt like chunks of ice.

Mr. Greggs lifted his arms for silence. He smiled around the room. "We have chosen the title for the school paper from all the wonderful titles that were submitted. Drum roll please." He glanced toward the ninth-grade boy at the drums and smiled.

The drum rolled and stopped abruptly.

"The winning title is . . . *Good News Weekly*!" He waited until the clapping and shouting stopped before he continued. "We chose that because we have a weekly newspaper and we put out good news. Marcie Gathier from seventh grade submitted that title. Will you stand, Marcie?"

Marcie stood and everyone applauded. Wren forced herself to clap.

After the meeting Wren walked out of the room, alone in the crowd. When she heard her name, though, she looked up to find Miss Brewster and

Mr. Abram just inches ahead of her.

"Wren handed in a wonderful article that she wrote all by herself," Miss Brewster was saying to Mr. Abram. Wren wanted to run from them, but she couldn't push through the crowd. "It was one of the best I've ever read. It's a real heartwarming story. I'd like to see her get a special award for finding such a story and for writing it."

Wren froze. She dare not let that happen! But how could she stop it?"

Miss Brewster glanced back, saw Wren and smiled. "I was just telling Mr. Abram that we should give you a special award for your story."

"Oh, no," said Wren in a tiny voice.

"I think we should plan on doing just that," said Mr. Abram. He smiled at Wren, but she couldn't smile back. He cocked his brow questioningly, but she couldn't speak.

In panic she fled from the school, ran all the way home, and burst into her dad's office.

Sam looked up in surprise, then slowly stood up and walked around his desk to Wren. "What is it, Wren?"

Tears streamed down her face. "I did something terrible, Dad!"

"Not you, Wren."

"Yes, yes, I did!" Between gasps for air she told him about the story, about deciding to take it back and then about her decision to leave it in even when she knew she was wrong. "What am I going to do now?"

"Wren, you already know that God loves you and you know that you only need to ask to be forgiven."

"I know, but I disobeyed God on purpose!"

"I'm so sorry, honey. I know you must be hurting. But even when you sin on purpose God is willing to forgive you if you ask. He loves you that much. You know not to disobey again. I know you'll remember that." Sam sat down in his big chair and pulled Wren onto his knees.

"When you accepted Christ as your Savior, God became your heavenly Father." Sam gently ruffled his daughter's hair. "And He loves you even more than I do. Your part now is to make the decision to do the right thing. God can't force you to do right. He can't force you to tell Miss Brewster what you did. It's your choice. But your decision will affect you. If you choose the wrong thing, you'll leave yourself open for Satan to attack you again. You don't want that to happen. If you ask Jesus to forgive you and you take back the story, you'll be free of the dark cloud over you."

Wren sniffed hard and her chin quivered as she looked up at her dad. "I want to take back the story. I will—but I don't know if I can! I don't want Neil to have a better story."

"Wren, don't let that stop you from doing the right thing."

"But it does."

"Wren, God will never let you face a temptation that is more than you can overcome. When a temptation to do wrong is put in your way, God offers you help to overcome it. But you must accept His help."

"But Neil's story will be better than mine!"

"Does it really matter, Wren?" Sam tightened his arm around her. "You don't want to disobey God just to write a better story than your brother . . . do you?"

"I guess not."

"Let God help you overcome the temptation, honey."

Wren thought about it a long time.

"I don't want to disobey and I don't want to lie about my story. I accept God's help." She sniffed hard and wiped a tear off her cheek. "I can't do it on my own, though."

Sam hugged her firmly. "None of us can, Wren."

"I'm afraid, Dad."

"Afraid?"

"To face Miss Brewster with the truth."

Sam smiled. "Wren, God loves you so much that He'll help you obey and He'll give you the courage to tell Miss Brewster. You are never alone, Wren. God is always, always with you."

Wren leaned her head against Dad's broad shoulder. "I'm glad I have two fathers—you and God."

"I am, too, Wren. Let's talk to our heavenly Father right now."

"Yeah, let's do, Dad."

"Father, thank you for the love and courage that you've given Wren."

Wren's eyes filled with tears as Dad prayed. When he finished she said, "Heavenly Father, forgive me for disobeying you. I am sorry. Help me not to ever do this again. I love you. Thank you for giving me a good dad who helps me. And thank you for Neil. I want to write a better story than he does, but I won't do wrong to do it. And I'll be happy for him if his really is better than mine."

An hour later Wren stood with her dad in Miss Brewster's living room. It made Wren feel funny to be in her teacher's house.

"When your father called, he said you have something to tell me, Wren," said Miss Brewster gently. "Is there a problem I can help you with?"

Wren took a deep breath. Instead of feeling full of panic, peace filled her. She looked right into Miss Brewster's eyes and told her what she'd done and that she was very sorry.

Miss Brewster took Wren's hand in hers. "It took a lot of courage for you to come to me. Thank you for doing it. And because you did, I'll accept your apology. We'll let the matter drop here. I'm sorry the story isn't true. You have a talent to write fiction, Wren. You should pursue it. But for this assignment it must be non-fiction. You still have until Tuesday afternoon to hand in your article, Wren. I think you can do it. I'm sure you'll be able to find something true to write."

Wren nodded. "We will, Miss Brewster. I promise. I'll work with my group and we'll write a good story—and this time it will be true." Wren smiled at Miss Brewster and Dad and they smiled back.

13.
The Missing Pig

Wren walked into the house with Dad close behind her. For the first time in days she felt like herself again. She was glad Miss Brewster had been so kind.

Neil walked out of the living room, a partly eaten peanut butter and jelly sandwich in one hand and a glass of milk in the other. "Wren, Mrs. Thomkins called you a few minutes ago. She said to call her back the minute you walk in."

"Thanks, Neil." Love for Neil rose up inside her and she smiled at him.

He grinned at her. "Anything for a lowly fifth grader."

"Neil," Dad said in his warning voice.

"Sorry." Neil winked at Wren and she could see he really was teasing her and that he didn't honestly think she was just a lowly fifth grader.

"That doesn't bother me as much any more," said Wren. "I know you're teasing."

"I am," said Neil. "But I'll quit if it hurts you."

"Thanks." She smiled at Neil and he offered her a bite of his sandwich, but she shook her head. "I'd better make this call." She ran to the phone and Mrs. Thomkins answered on the first ring.

"Wren!" Mrs. Thomkins sounded relieved. "I need you to come right over. Mrs. Banner is here and she's frantic. She won't tell me what's wrong. She said she has to talk to you. I called you for her because she doesn't have a phone. And she's trembling so badly that she couldn't dial your number."

Wren gripped the receiver tighter. Had someone discovered Suie? Or had something terrible happened to the pig? "I'll be right there. Tell Mrs. Banner not to worry." Wren dropped the receiver in place and silently prayed for Mrs. Banner, Mrs. Thomkins, and even Suie. It felt great to be able to talk with God without the black cloud that had surrounded her.

Gaining permission quickly from her dad, it was just a few minutes later when she stopped her bike outside Mrs. Thomkins's house. Before she could walk to the door, it burst open and Mrs. Banner ran out, her hair flying all over. Her eyes were wild. She gripped Wren's arm and her fingers bit through Wren's jacket into her arms.

"She's gone! Wren, she's gone! I've looked all over and I can't find her."

"Suie?"

"Yes! Oh, Wren. I can't live without her. You helped me before and you helped Mrs. Thomkins. Please, please help me find Suie."

"I will. I'll call Tim and Bess."

Several minutes later Bess and then Tim rode into Mrs. Banner's yard.

"What's the secret?" asked Bess.

"Is it the pig?" asked Tim.

"Pig?" Bess squealed and looked around with wide eyes.

"It's Suie," said Mrs. Banner, tugging her coat around her to keep out the chilly wind. "She disappeared about four this afternoon. I don't ever let her out during the day, but she ran out when I opened the door. She was here in the yard one minute and the next thing I knew, she wasn't."

"We'll find her, Mrs. Banner." Wren patted the woman's arm. "We'll get her back to you."

"But what if someone sees her?" Mrs. Banner's face turned as gray as the sky.

Bess stepped forward with her arms crossed and her brows furrowed. "I want to know why I'm here. What's going on? I thought I was going to help with a newspaper or something. Isn't that the case you're working on, Wren?"

"I solved the case of the missing papers, Bess. This is something else." Wren took a deep breath. "Mrs. Banner has a pet pig."

"Pet pig!"

"A pet pig named Suie. And she's gone."

"Suie is a secret because pigs aren't allowed in the city," said Tim. "She belongs to Mrs. Banner and has been her pet since Suie was born."

Bess wrinkled her nose. "I never heard of having a pig for a pet."

Wren hadn't either but all she said was, "Let's go look for Suie." Wren assigned them places to search. Mrs. Banner hurried away, but before Wren, Tim, and Bess could go anywhere Paula Gantz rode up.

"What's going on here?" asked Paula. "Where's Sean? Is this a meeting for our newspaper group?"

"No," said Wren.

"We're going to find a pet . . . . "

Before Bess could finish Wren grabbed her and hushed her. "Paula, this is none of your business. We're here to help Mrs. Banner."

"Help with what? Who's Mrs. Banner?" Paula looked around suspicously. A car drove past. Down the street a man shouted in anger. "What pet are you going to find?"

"Mrs. Banner's pet," said Tim. "If you're going to stick around, then join in and help us look. It might take us hours, but you don't mind that do you? You like to work for no reward just to help others."

Wren hid a smile. She knew just what Tim was doing.

Paula tugged down her jacket. "I have to get home right now. I don't want to find a pet for anyone."

"Good," said Wren.

Paula looked closely at her. "I know you're keeping another secret from me but I'll bet I find out what it is."

"I know the secret," said Bess with a smug look on her face.

"Bess!" cried Wren.

"What?" Bess turned wide, innocent eyes on Wren.

"Are you staying or going, Paula?" asked Tim.

"Going!"

Smiling, Wren watched Paula ride away. "Let's go! We'll meet back here in a half hour."

"Aren't we going to pray first?" asked Bess.

Wren squeezed Bess's hand and smiled. "Sure, we'll pray first."

"I'll pray," said Tim. He stepped beside the girls. "Heavenly Father, we know you care about Mrs. Banner and about Suie. Help us find Suie right away. And thank you for letting us help."

A few minutes later Wren rode her bike down the streets that she'd chosen. Maybe she'd find Suie again and then she'd tell Jason Cole all about it and maybe bring another giggle from him. Saturday morning she'd watched Jason with Suie and she'd heard another sound from Jason. It had startled him so much that he'd stopped playing with Suie.

He'd turned to Wren excitedly and had pointed to his mouth.

Wren thought of that again and smiled. It was funny to think that two people could love a pig as much as Jason and Mrs. Banner did.

Wren rode around a tricycle, stopped and looked at her watch. It was time to go back and she hadn't found Suie. "But we'll find her! We will!" She nodded as she turned and rode back to Mrs. Banner's house.

A police car stood at the curb. Wren's stomach tightened. Had something terrible happened?

Just then, from the back of the house, Suie squealed as if she was being hurt. Fear pricked Wren's skin. She dropped her bike and dashed around to find Bess, Tim, Mrs. Banner and a police officer standing around Suie. Paula Gantz stood to one side of the group with a smug look on her face.

"You can't keep a pig in town," said the officer.

"But she's my baby!" cried Mrs. Banner, touching Suie's head.

"What happened?" asked Wren.

"Paula told," said Tim, glaring at Paula.

Paula made a face at Tim. "And I'm glad I did!"

Bess wiped a tear off her cheek. "I found Suie and I didn't know Paula was following me. She saw Suie and she said she'd tell and I told her not to, but

114

she did!"

"I won't let you take Suie." Mrs. Banner dropped on her knees and wrapped her arms around the pig's neck. "If you take her, you have to take me." She turned an anguished face to Wren. "Help me, Wren! Help Suie!"

Wren stared helplessly at Mrs. Banner, trying to think of some way to help her.

The officer said, "I'm going to call for a truck to haul the pig away. I don't like to do this to you, Mrs. Banner, but it's the law."

"No!" Mrs. Banner burst into wild tears.

Wren stepped up to the officer. "My name is Wren House. What is your name?"

The officer frowned down at her. He was tall and broad. "Officer Jake Ezra."

Wren lifted her head and squared her shoulders. Butterflies fluttered in her stomach, but she didn't let them show. "Lorrene House is my mother and she's a lawyer. Will you give me time to call her? She may be able to help us."

"That's a good idea, little girl. You go call your mother and I'll go call a truck." He turned and strode toward his waiting car.

Wren dashed to Mrs. Thomkins's house and knocked on her door. There was no answer.

"She's not home," said Tim. "I wanted to call Adam, but Mrs. Banner said that Mrs. Thomkins had an appointment and had to leave just after you called us."

115

"How about the neighbor over there?"

"He wouldn't let me use his phone."

Wren ran around the house for her bike, then stopped. "It'll take too long to ride home and then come back with Mom. I'll see if the officer will put a call through!"

"I don't think he will," said Tim.

"I'll ask." Wren ran to the car just as the officer closed his car door.

He turned to Wren with a questioning look.

"I can't get to a phone and I need you to call my mom." Wren caught her breath and locked her icy hands together in front of her. A leaf blew across her foot and stopped against the car's front tire.

"I can't do that."

"Her dad is Sam House the detective and her mom really is a lawyer," said Tim. "They both will help Mrs. Banner if you'll make the call."

"I don't know." Officer Ezra pulled off his hat and scratched his head. A smile tugged at the corner of his wide mouth. He had dark hair and nice eyes.

"It will save time," said Wren. "I could ride home and get Mom, but it would be much quicker to call her and have her drive over."

"You're right." Officer Ezra turned back to his car and reached inside.

Wren listened as he talked into the mike. She moved closer to Tim, her heart in her mouth. Would Mom know just how important it was to

116

come right over?

"She'll come," whispered Tim.

Wren nodded. "She will." She had to!

Several minutes later Lorrene House drove up. With a glad cry Wren ran to her.

"Mrs. Banner needs your help, Mom."

"So I understand." Lorrene shook her head. "Wren, I don't know how you manage to get involved in such strange things. But lead me to Mrs. Banner and her pig."

"Right around the house." Wren caught Mom's hand. "Thanks, Mom. I knew you'd come. I know you can help Mrs. Banner keep her pig."

Lorrene stopped. "Hold it, Wren. I can't help her keep her pig. It's against the law for a pig to live in town because of the smell and the damage it does."

"But, Mom!"

"It's the law, Wren."

"What about Mrs. Banner? It'll break her heart!" Great tears filled Wren's eyes and slowly slipped down her cheeks.

14.
Suie

Wren sniffed hard and wiped away her tears. "Mom, there must be a way for Mrs. Banner to keep her pig."

"There is no way she can keep the pig in town. But we'll find a way for her to keep the pig."

"You will?"

"Let's go talk to Officer Ezra, shall we?" Lorrene bent down and kissed Wren's cheek. "We'll find a way."

Wren's heart leaped as she walked beside her mom.

Lorrene stepped forward with her hand out. "Officer Ezra, I'm Lorrene House. I came to help Mrs. Banner."

They shook hands and Officer Ezra said, "I don't know what good you can do, but I'm glad you came."

Mrs. Banner looked up from where she sat with Suie. "They want to take Suie, but I won't let them."

"Mom will help you," said Wren confidently.

"I bet she can't," taunted Paula.

"Don't, Paula!" Bess and Tim said together.

"Go home, Paula," said Lorrene in a firm voice. "You're upsetting my client and I can't allow that."

Paula swallowed hard, stood undecidedly, then ran to her bike and rode home.

"I can't live without Suie, Mrs. House," said Mrs. Banner in a strangled voice. Her face was ashen. Her pants and jacket were soiled from Suie.

Suie grunted and tried to get away, but Mrs. Banner held on tightly to the collar around Suie's thick neck.

"I'll do all I can to help you," said Lorrene with a smile. She turned back to the officer. "I want permission for my client to keep her pig with her until she can make suitable arrangements to move her."

Officer Ezra rubbed the back of his neck. "Well, I don't know."

Lorrene looked Officer Ezra right in the eye. "I can call Judge Mosher."

After a long time the officer nodded. "All right. She has until tomorrow morning."

"Twenty four hours."

"All right. Twenty four hours. But that's all. I mean it! I'll cancel the truck." Officer Ezra strode to his car and drove away.

Wren could barely stand still. So far Mom had won, but what would happen next?

Lorrene rested her hand on Mrs. Banner's shoulder. "Let's go inside and talk, shall we?"

Mrs. Banner stood and her bones creaked. She rubbed her lower back with one hand and held Suie's collar with the other. "I can't pay you much, you know."

"We'll discuss that later." Lorrene turned to Bess and Tim. "Run on home, kids. Wren will let you know how it turns out. Wren, you may come inside with us."

Wren smiled in relief. She had to hear what Mom and Mrs. Banner discussed.

A few minutes later Mrs. Banner turned Suie into the room that had been set aside for her. Then Mrs. Banner led Lorrene and Wren to the living room and they sat on the couch while she sat on a chair across from them. The room was clean, but smelled terrible because of Suie.

Lorrene crossed her legs and smoothed her skirt over her knees. She acted as if there was no pig and no pig smell. "Mrs. Banner, you know the law won't allow you to keep the pig in town. Is there someone in the country who could keep Suie for you?"

"No!" Mrs. Banner looked ready to cry.

"Suie can't stay here," said Lorrene in a soft voice. "We must think of somewhere to keep Suie so that you can be with her as often as you like. Can't you think of any such place?"

"No!" Mrs. Banner shook her head hard.

Wren moved restlessly. "What about your old farm, Mrs. Banner? There's room there. And Jason loves Suie and Suie loves Jason."

Mrs. Banner sat very still, her hand at her wrinkled throat. Finally she nodded. "My old farm. Yes. Jason does love Suie and she loves him. Yes."

"Tell me about it," said Lorrene.

Mrs. Banner and Wren took turns talking about the farm and about Jason. Wren ended by saying, "I think Suie will help Jason talk again. And if she's there all the time, it'll be even better for Jason."

"That's wonderful," said Lorrene.

Mrs. Banner pushed herself up. "I'll call Simon Cole right now from Mrs. Thomkins's house. If he won't agree to letting Suie stay there, then we'll have to think of something else."

Lorrene touched Mrs. Banner's arm and smiled. "Let me call him for you. That's my job."

"Thank you. I might start blubbering and embarrass myself and him."

"If it's agreeable, we'll take Suie out tomorrow afternoon," said Lorrene. "That will give you a while to be alone with her."

"I'd like that."

"Why did you move from the farm if you loved it so much?" asked Lorrene.

"I was forced to."

"She was supposed to live there all the rest of her life," said Wren.

Mrs. Banner finished telling the story with a few questions thrown in now and then from Lorrene. "I'd move back there in a flash if I could and I'd rent this house out again." Mrs. Banner sighed loud and long. "But happy endings don't happen very often in real life."

"We'll see about that, too," said Lorrene with a smile.

The next afternoon Wren rode to the farm in the pickup with Mrs. Banner. Lorrene followed in her car.

Mrs. Banner pulled up beside the barn. Her face was pale when she turned to Wren. "Are you sure I should do this?"

"I'm sure, Mrs. Banner. Don't be frightened."

"I'm not frightened. But lonely. For Suie."

"But Mr. Cole said you could come over every day all day long."

Mrs. Banner nodded. "I know, but it's just not the same." With a sigh she opened the door and stepped to the ground. Suie grunted in the back of the pickup.

Wren jumped out just as Jason and Levi ran out of the house with their parents following behind. Wren saw the joy on Jason's face and she knew Mrs. Banner saw it too.

Simon Cole helped Mrs. Banner prop the ramp in place, then stood back as Suie walked down, grunting and squealing.

"You're home again, Suie," said Mrs. Banner with a catch in her voice.

Suie rooted in the dirt in the driveway, then lifted her head. She saw Jason, grunted and ran to him, pushing her snout against his chest.

Jason giggled and his family gasped in surprise.

Wren felt as if she'd burst with happiness. She looked up at Mom and smiled.

"A happy ending," whispered Lorrene.

Suddenly everyone turned around as one clear word rang out.

"Suie," said Jason.

Wren's eyes prickled with tears as Jason's dad lifted him high in his arms and both his parents kissed him.

"You can talk again!" his mom exclaimed.

"I knew you'd talk again, Jason." Levi added excitedly.

Mrs. Banner said, "I'm glad I brought Suie to live here. This just made it all worthwhile."

Simon Cole stood his son down and Jason ran to Suie again.

"Mrs. Banner," he said, tears still in his eyes, "Mrs. House explained to us about the promise that this should be your home all of your life."

"We didn't know about that promise," said Wanda Cole.

Mrs. Banner looked from one to the other.

"If you want, you can move back in with us.

There's an extra bedroom and bathroom just off the kitchen that can be yours." Simon smiled. "I know it's not as private as having the entire place to yourself, but we don't want to move back to the city."

"Could we share the home?" asked Wanda Cole, holding a hand out to Mrs. Banner. "We're willing to try, if you are."

Mrs. Banner swallowed hard. "The house was always too big for me. I'd be happy to share it with you."

"You can move in as soon as you want," said Simon.

"Thank you."

"Look, Mom!" shouted Jason from across the yard where he was playing with Suie. "Suie's doing a trick."

"He said a whole sentence!" cried Levi.

The Cole family ran to Jason with glad cries. Mrs. Banner started forward, then turned back.

"Mrs. House, thank you for all of your help. And, Wren, you're a good friend to me and Suie both. Thank you."

"We were glad to help," said Lorrene.

"I'll come see you and Suie when I can," said Wren.

A few minutes later Wren rode beside Lorrene back to town. The bright sun shone through the car window. "What a happy ending, Mom!"

"The entire episode would make a wonderful

124

story," said Lorrene.

Wren's heart leaped. "It would!"

"It might even be the best story in the school paper."

Wren tipped back her head and laughed. "I think so too, but even if it's not the best, it'll be a story that will make people laugh and cry and be glad for miracles from God."

"That's right, Wren."

"I have a lot of people to tell this story to. Or maybe I'll let them read it in the *Good News Weekly*."

"I'm proud of you, Wren House."

"Thanks, Mom. I'm proud of you, too." Wren stretched over and kissed Mom's soft cheek. "I love you, Mom."

Be sure to look for other books in *The Wren House Mystery Series.*